INTIMATES

Other books by David Huddle

STORIES

A Dream with No Stump Roots in It
Only the Little Bone
The High Spirits

POEMS

Paper Boy
Stopping by Home
The Nature of Yearning

ESSAYS

The Writing Habit

INTIMATES

A Book of Stories

David Huddle

DAVID R. GODINE, PUBLISHER
Boston

First published in 1993 by
David R. Godine, Publisher, Inc.
Horticultural Hall
300 Massachusetts Avenue
Boston, Massachusetts 02115

Library of Congress Cataloguing in Publication Data
Huddle, David, 1942–
Intimates : a book of stories / David Huddle.—1st ed.
p. cm.
ISBN 0-87923-933-6
I. Title.
PS3558.U28I56 1993   92-39279
813'.54—dc20   CIP

FIRST EDITION
Printed in the United States of America

Acknowledgments

These stories appeared, in slightly different versions,
in the following periodicals and anthologies:

"Collision" in *Shenandoah*

"The Page" in *New Virginia Review*

"Scotland" in *New England Review*

"Mister Mister" in *Story*

"Night" in *Louder Than Words: A Second Collection,*
Vintage Books

"The Hearing" in *New Madrid*

"The Meeting of the Tisdale Fellows"
in *New Virginia Review*

"The Reunion Joke" in *Glimmer Train Stories*

"The Short Flight" in *Elvis in Oz: New Stories
from the Hollins Creative Writing Program,*
University Press of Virginia

"Trouble at the Home Office" in *The Southern Review*

"Henry Lagoon" and "Little Sawtooth"
in *Colorado North Review*

For Alan Broughton and John Engels

"Yes, yes, yes, but what's the He and She of it?"
JAMES JOYCE

INTIMATES

Night

"HELP ME WITH THIS, baby girl," my father told me. He was turning on all the lights in our living room. This was the year we lived in Seattle, the year I started becoming aware of how much he drank. I must have been around eleven. We had a rambling house with a huge window that looked out over Puget Sound, a window that was almost the whole wall of our living room. I remember feeling good about the lights I could see coming on down there around the bay, but feeling anxious about my father wanting so many lights on in the house.

He and I were there alone. He and my mom had had a fight a couple of days before this evening, and she'd flown back to New York for a week or so. Randy, my brother, and my father had had a fight earlier that afternoon. Randy had stormed out with my father screaming at him to come back that very minute and Randy screaming back at him. When my brother was thirteen and fourteen, he and my father fought like that pretty often. This was a Saturday, I think; they mostly fought on weekends.

I'd hung around the living room, sort of keeping an eye on my father, because I'd learned that he didn't like being surprised by any of us coming upon him unexpectedly, especially if he was in the pantry pouring a drink or in the kitchen getting ice. He didn't even like it if you were just sitting in the living room, looking at a magazine or listening to a record, and he walked in on you without already knowing you were there.

I'd kept meaning to tell Randy about this trick I had of keeping Dad in sight, or keeping him aware that I was around, because that way I didn't surprise him and set him off. Lots of times he'd walk in on Randy who'd have a glass of milk and a plate of cookies or a sandwich and his school stuff strewn all around the sofa and coffee table; then my father would start yelling at him for being a slob and a deadbeat, and they'd be into it again.

This was also around the time that I caught on to how I could use my tennis training to sidetrack him from drinking so much and picking on Randy and my mom. If I could get him out on the court with me—we had an old-fashioned red-clay court at that house and this Japanese gardener who kept it in perfect condition—if I could get my father out there with me, and get him moving enough to work up a sweat, then he usually drank a lot less and didn't pick on us nearly as much.

But this particular morning, he and I had had only about an hour's workout before he had to go downtown to have lunch with some people from his company, and when he came home that afternoon, he went straight to the pantry. Then he ran into Randy in the living room and started yelling at him, Randy stormed out, and I spent the rest of the afternoon sort of softly stalking my father around the house, now and then saying, "How you doing, Dad?" or "Do you want anything from the kitchen, Dad?"

My father had gotten quiet about half an hour before he turned on the lights, but that wasn't unusual. I could tell from his facial expression that he knew I was around and that he wasn't angry at me. He had been standing at the windows, looking one way and then another. Then he began switching on every lamp in the living room, and I knew something strange was happening. "Now go turn on the lights in your bedroom, baby girl," he told me. I suddenly understood that he was afraid of something.

I had probably seen more than most eleven-year-old girls had. Our parents had taken my brother and me with them on trips to Europe, the Philippines, Hong Kong, Japan, and Australia, and we'd lived in London, New York, Houston, and now Seattle. I'd seen my father angry and happy and even depressed, but I hadn't ever seen him afraid of anything or anybody. I did as he'd instructed me, turned on the lights in my bedroom, even the lamp on my dresser that almost never got turned on. When I came back to the living room, I could hear him moving through the rest of the house, turning on lights, I supposed. Momentarily he came back in with me and asked if the drapes were open in my room. I told him I thought they were.

"I think they're afraid of light," he told me. "At least that's what I'm counting on."

"Who, Dad?" I asked him. Usually he didn't like being questioned, and so I made my voice sound friendly and interested, as if we were having a little conversation about a football team he'd read about in the newspaper.

He was on his way to the pantry to get a fresh drink, but he made a gesture back toward the living room window and said, "Go look for yourself."

I moved to the big window and stood there for a long time, looking out one way and then another, as I'd seen my father do. At first I'd been curious to see what might be out there. I imagined animals of some sort—maybe wolves or coyotes I thought, since this was the West—and then I imagined gangsters. But I saw nothing except the terraces of our front yard, the lights of the neighbors' houses, and then the usual pretty lights around the bay far in the distance. I really did look hard out there until I knew for certain that I wasn't going to see whatever it was my father was seeing.

When I turned back to the living room, he was staring at me, and I knew he had been staring at my back while I stood there. He had brought a bottle of Canadian Club in from the pantry and set it on the floor beside his chair. He was sweating, and he had loosened his tie. My father is the only man I know who wears a coat and tie to relax in. He worked then for an import-export company that was known for its executives' wearing good clothes; my father took pride in being the one who set the standards for everyone else in the company. Every year after Christmas he bought half a dozen new suits and at least that many sports jackets and trouser sets. He had literally hundreds of ties. For me to see him that night sitting there in his shirt sleeves with his tie loose was the same as for somebody else to see her father stripped down to his underwear.

"Put on some music, baby girl," he told me. I must have given him a questioning look because then he spoke to me impatiently—as if I should have known this all along—"They're afraid of music."

Music seemed like a good idea to me. I started to put on

Peter, Paul & Mary, because that was my favorite record in his and my mom's collection—it had belonged to her in college, I think—but he saw which one I'd picked and told me, "Not that one."

"What would you like to hear, Dad?" Again, I was careful to keep my voice normal and friendly, not to upset him. When he didn't answer right away, I turned to look at him. He had his eyes on the window. I waited awhile and then said very softly, "Dad?"

He jerked his head around toward me and shouted at me, "You'd better get a record on that stereo right away, or you're going to have a lot of trouble come and visit you."

That about trouble coming to visit was something he said both when he was kidding and when he really meant it. I'd learned to know which it was by the tone of his voice. This time he definitely meant it. "Overture 1812" seemed to me the best choice because that was what he listened to sometimes after he and my mom had had a fight. Maybe for that reason, I'd gotten so I hated it, especially the really loud parts where my father always stood up and waved his arms and pointed like he was the conductor of the orchestra. When I put it on and came back to the sofa to sit down, my father nodded at me, picked up the bottle of Canadian Club, and poured himself another drink from it. He sipped, nodded, and told me, "I think we've got a chance, baby girl."

When that side of the record finished playing, he looked at me, nodding toward the stereo. I got up to change it, then started to slip off to my bedroom—mostly because it was that last part of "Overture 1812" that I hated the most. "Where you going, baby girl?" my father asked.

"To put my pajamas on," I told him, which was a smart

thing for me to say. He wouldn't have liked it if I'd just said, "To my room." I remember thinking I'd gotten pretty smart about the way I could deal with him.

"Hurry on back," he said. "I'll worry about you if you're gone too long."

He'd made his voice sound sweet, but I knew that he was lying to me, that it was himself he was worried about, that he didn't want to be by himself. That was a first, too. I'd gotten used to thinking of my father as temperamental and unfair and a bully lots of times. But those seemed his due as a father and as a man who had a high-pressure job and made a lot of money. So far as I knew—though, being only eleven, what could I really know about him?—he hadn't lied to me before. He'd made me do lots of things I didn't want to do, he'd even slapped me a few times, but I'd never been aware of his trying to get me to do something by lying to me.

"I will, Dad," I said, and even as I spoke those words, my father seemed to be shrinking in my mind. You know how when you're little, your parents seem huge to you, and maybe with my father I'd hung on too long to that way of thinking about him. Actually, he was a pretty normal-sized man, 5′ 11″ and 165 or 175 pounds, and so maybe what was happening as I thought about it in my room, changing into my pajamas and bathrobe, was just that I was starting to see him for what he was, a regular person. But I remember feeling sad about him and worried. The whole house seemed weird because of having all the lights on, which made even my own room seem like not my room.

I took a chance and tried to stay in there until the record was over, but pretty soon, my father knocked on the door and called out, "Hurry it up, Angela." So I went out right away. He didn't use my name unless he was mad or just about to get that way. He had gone to stand at the window again, and I was glad he was doing that instead of conducting the music. I sat on the sofa, trying to think my brother back into the house. Because I'd read some article somewhere about "The Powers of the Mind," I was always trying to think something into happening. It didn't work for getting Randy back home that night; he'd gone to stay with one of his friends from school. But at least it did give me something to do while I sat up with my dad.

When the music ended, my father looked at me and gave that little movement of his head that meant he wanted me to put on another record. I started to ask him what he wanted to hear next, but I changed my mind. Somehow I liked it better without having to hear him say anything and without my having to say anything to him. So I just started with the first record on the left-hand side of his and my mom's collection and figured if he kept on making me play records for him, I'd go through them that way, so as not to have to think about which one to play next.

That was the longest night of my life. My father woke me up a couple of times to go and turn the record over or put on another one. But now that I think back over it, I doubt that it was all that late when my father finally passed out—maybe at the outside latest, it was midnight. But at the time it seemed like he and I had fallen through the bottom of the night and it wouldn't ever get to be morning again.

What finally happened was that I became aware of a long stretch of silence and snapped open my eyes. My father was slumped over in his chair, asleep with his mouth open. For a moment I thought about trying to move him into the bedroom, but then I realized that with him asleep, I was finally free to do whatever I wanted to do. I got up and turned off the stereo and went all through the house turning off lights and closing drapes. I took my father's glass into the kitchen and rinsed it out, and I put what was left of his bottle of Canadian Club back into the pantry. I wrote my brother a note and taped it to the outside of the back door where I knew he would come if he came back at all that night; I told him to come tap on my window, and I'd let him in the house. I checked to see that all the doors were locked, and I took a last look at my father. I could tell that he wasn't dead or sick or anything, he was just very soundly asleep. Again, I was tempted to try to move him to the sofa, or just to loosen his tie a little more, but I really didn't want to touch him. I could just imagine waking him up and his saying, "Put on another record, baby girl."

I'd already been to my room to turn off the ceiling light and the light on the dresser, and I'd even straightened up my bed and put my clothes away. I didn't usually do things like that, because we'd always had a maid who took care of my room on weekdays. But it was Saturday, and I knew I wanted my room to be exactly right when I finally was able to go to bed that night. First I went to the bathroom, then I walked slowly into my room where I'd left the bedside light on, the last light that was on in the whole house. I remember thinking to myself as I took off my bathrobe and carefully hung it on its hook inside the closet door, "I've been a good girl tonight." Pulling down my covers and swinging my body up into bed and turning off the light, I was thinking, "Nobody knows it, but tonight I've been the best girl anybody could be."

My sheets were that cool temperature that makes you curl up and shiver and think about how warm you're soon going to be and how sweet it will feel to fall asleep. All of a sudden I was thinking about my mom, about how not so many years earlier, she'd helped me learn how to read; she'd been so excited when I started being able to sound out the words in a book, and when we finished reading one of those books like *Frog and Toad*, we'd both be excited, and she'd give me a big hug, and I'd feel like the smartest kid anywhere.

All through that night with my father, I'd avoided thinking about my mom, the way you're afraid to let anybody see the one thing you care about the most in the world because their seeing it might spoil it for you. I must have thought my dad would somehow ruin the way I thought about my mom if I thought about her when I was out there with him. But when I was there in my room, curled up in my bed, I could think about her all I wanted to, all the way into sleep. I thought about my mom's clothes. I knew them almost as well as she did, and though I hadn't told her, I had my own favorites among her underwear and slips and dresses and blouses and sweaters. I thought about her getting dressed to go out to a party. I thought about her putting on a new silk blouse she'd gotten for Christmas from my grandparents. I loved my mom so much that night, and she wasn't even in the same house with me.

Scotland

WHEN I CAME HOME FROM SCHOOL, I knew my dad
was in the house, even though there was absolute quiet everywhere. This was years ago, when we lived in London and I was
thirteen and trying to get used to going to school at St. Cather-
ine's Academy where they made us wear flannel skirts and
knee socks. My dad was mostly living with his mistress, as my
mom called her. He had stopped paying our cook and maid; so
that day there wasn't even any noise coming from the kitchen.
My dad drank, and he had always been a very tense man. Even
when he was in a good mood, you didn't want to startle him,
or come up on him by surprise. So after I got myself a snack, I
went very quietly to my room, which was down the hall from
my mom's room, and took off my skirt and blouse and dropped
them to the floor as I always did but still being careful not to
make much noise.

All the while I was putting on my jeans and sweat shirt and

eating my crackers and cheese, I kept imagining that I could hear murmuring voices from her room. I lay down on the bed to read and maybe take a nap, but I also wanted to be as quiet as I could to see if I really was hearing them talking. I even held my breath, but the quieter I was, the more my imagination seemed to be playing tricks on me. One minute I'd be certain I heard my father speaking actual words, things like "I have every right" and "You don't know," and once I even thought I heard my mom say my name, "Angela," in this real tight voice. But then the next minute I'd be just as certain that I wasn't hearing anything except my own blood beating in my ears.

After awhile I think I must have dozed off or gone into this trance or something, but I seemed to know that it was getting dark outside. Then I was aware of my dad standing in the hallway just outside my doorway. He stood there for an unusually long time, and while he did, I became more and more alert. By the time he had started down the steps, a little sweat had broken onto my forehead.

Probably he opened and closed the front door as softly as he could, but I was so tense waiting for him to leave that it sounded like a small explosion when he finally did shut it behind him. A second later, my mom screamed for me to come to her room.

She was in her white dressing gown and as pale as I'd ever seen her. In there by the bay windows was a small table with a white tablecloth on it. When we had first moved into that house, she and my dad had liked having breakfast in their room on weekends. My mom still kept a small vase of fresh flowers on it most of the time. She explained that about an hour ago my dad had come into the room, gone to the table, moved the vase of flowers aside, taken a pistol from his jacket pocket and set it in the middle of the table, sat down, and invited her to join him.

I understood why she never thought of refusing the invitation. My dad wasn't a joker. If he wanted you to do something, you did it. I thought that my father would have used that pistol if my mom hadn't done what he wanted.

She said that he talked very quietly with her, telling her how she must stop the divorce procedure, how then he would re-hire the cook and the maid, and how then he would give up one of his usual nights with his mistress to be with us. She said he was pleasant and charming; he didn't even ask her to agree with him or say yes to anything. He simply described to her what she was going to do and what they were going to do. Then he stood up and as if it had been a trinket or a pocket watch, slipped the pistol back into his jacket. He gave her a peck on the cheek and said goodbye.

She said that even as pleasant as he was, every second of the conversation she expected him to pick up the gun and level it at her forehead.

She wanted me to tell her what I thought she should do. I persuaded her to call Michael Land and ask his advice. Michael Land was a lawyer there in London and was also my mother's first cousin. She called him while I was sitting there with her. On the phone, Michael told her he would arrange a little trip for us to get away and to allow my dad to cool off a bit.

Michael Land was my favorite relative. He was elegant and cheerful and so confident that he made you believe he could do anything. The next day at noon on the dot, he picked us up in a taxi; he even helped the driver load the car. My mom and I pestered Michael, but he wouldn't tell us where we going until we were in Heathrow and walking to the gate. Once we got there, we didn't need him to tell us: it was a Dan Air flight, and we were going to Scotland.

Before we boarded, Michael talked very quietly with my mom and gave her a portfolio. He thought that since my dad might try to find us, it would be best if we didn't stay in any one place for too long. He had wanted to arrange a tour for us, but a commercial one would have been too easy for my dad to track down. Then he'd remembered that my mom had done some magazine writing before she was married, and Michael had a friend who arranged tours of the whisky distilleries for American journalists. We were to join a group starting out from Inverness the next day.

I remember how excited we were on the plane, my mom as giddy and pleased with herself as if she'd just landed a terrific new job. I remember noticing how young she seemed. My mom was small and blond with high cheekbones and a perfect little nose, and her eyes were this special brownish-green color. I've never seen anybody with eyes like my mom's. She pulled out *Dan Air Magazine* and started checking out the articles in it, "refreshing her professional judgment," she said in this mock haughty voice.

This was in late April. In London the weather had been summerish, warm enough at mid-day even to take off your sweater and try to get a little sun on your arms. But coming down the ramp at Inverness, with the cold rain driving into our faces, I thought of my dad. Though I didn't say anything about it, I could tell that my mom had lost some of her excitement over our adventure.

That night at dinner, she got to talking about how our lives were just about to undergo this drastic change and about how I had been so spoiled up until now. I finally had to tell her, "Mom, you're being very boring." I expected her to be irked, or maybe even to show a little hurt—nobody really likes to be told that they're boring—but the look she gave me was calculating, as if she were trying to estimate how much of a little girl I still was and how much of a grown-up.

The next morning, we took a cab back to the airport's main terminal to meet our tour's other people, who had just flown up from London. The lady in charge was a librarian/school-teacher kind of person named Alicia, who shook hands with each of us, then introduced us very properly to the others. James was a bald, very light-skinned black man, a flashy dresser and the editor of a magazine called *Contemporary Black Man*. The other two guys were with James. There was Mac, this arrogant New York city photographer, about half as good-looking as he thought he was. And then there was Larry, the model who was also the *CBM* man of the year.

Whereas James's skin was the color of coffee with a lot of milk in it, Larry's was a kind of powdery gray, like marble or granite. For a model, his clothes were sort of ordinary, though I thought they were stylish enough—designer jeans and cow-boy boots, a white turtleneck under a dark sweater, and a long gray overcoat with a big collar. When you first saw him, the first thing you thought wouldn't be that he was a model, or even that he was black. You would guess that he was somebody special. And on second look, you'd figure out that he was black, because you could see it in his features. Larry wasn't the handsomest man I'd ever seen—he was probably only about the fifth or sixth handsomest. But when I first saw him, I was just struck by the sight of him, the way you are when you see a race horse or a hawk up close.

We had one of those British-style "coaches," a bus about half the size of a Greyhound, with lots of extra seats that we filled up with luggage and Mac's photography equipment. Our driver was Mike, a Scot, a little square man, whose dialect was so pronounced that even Alicia seemed to have trouble understanding him; she sat up front so as to consult with him about our itinerary. My mom sat in the seat behind Mike and across from Alicia. James and Mac took the middle of the bus. I walked almost to the back before I took a seat. Larry took the one across the aisle from me. "Angela is your name?" he asked me. When I nodded, he asked me something about my school, but before I could answer him, he asked me if I wanted to sit with him.

His asking me that took my breath away so that I wasn't able to answer him, but I had no trouble moving my body over into the seat beside him. I know I was blushing from imagining how he would see me; my mom had made me wear a dress, and I had on a sweater. I'd grown an inch taller than my mom that year, but I still didn't have any hips or chest to speak of. I couldn't tell if he was thinking of me as a kid or a girl, but either way, I wanted to sit with him. Later on, Larry told me that he took my not saying anything as evidence of my being cool toward him. I never told him that I had been almost too thrilled to breathe, let alone squeeze any words out of myself.

We were traveling through gently rolling landscape that wasn't remarkable for anything except the deep green of the fields. The weather was gloomy, low gray clouds and rain swatting the windshield. It was the kind of day that would have put me to sleep in any other circumstance. But sitting in that bus seat beside Larry, I felt the exact opposite of sleepy. I wanted to see every single grass blade and neat little house and garden. I didn't want to touch him or him to touch me; in fact, I felt as if the molecules of my body were fitting more and more tightly, like a jigsaw puzzle that had finally been put together, and now somebody was pressing the pieces down on the table.

Our first stop was Brodie Castle. It had pretty trees and gardens around it, but from the outside, the thing really wasn't much to look at, just a big sandy-colored building. Getting off the bus, I made some sarcastic remarks about getting the tour off to a boring start with "Brodie the Boring" and things like that. I had just discovered how flexible the concept of boredom was—you could apply it to just about anything you didn't like—and so I liked designating big things, like a sixteenth-century Scottish castle, as boring.

But Larry, it turned out, couldn't have been more interested in the place and in Brodie himself, who greeted us at the castle door, wearing a kilt and a tweed jacket and a tie. Brodie had a big voice—he later told us he had worked as a professional actor in London—and he had black, curly hair, this huge nose, a jaw and lower lip that stuck out, and a kind of quarter-moon–shaped face. He insisted that we all call him merely Brodie—"Call me by the name of my place," he said, and you could tell he liked the sound of "Brodie of Brodie," which was what his nametag had typed on it.

All of a sudden James got the bright idea to have Larry pose with Brodie for a picture, and so for a little while, it was like being in the audience of a live TV show. Mac set up his cameras with this bemused air about him. James took on the role of the man in charge of everything. He gave directions for Larry and Mac to do what they obviously already intended to do, while he posed over to the side of the action, smoking and squinting and chattering away.

The first shots they set up were in the castle dining room, where the table was grandly set for twelve, except that there wasn't any silverware. Alicia and Mom and I stood together near the huge bay window of the room. My mom put her arm around my waist and asked me, "How's my girl?" I leaned my head on her shoulder and said that I was doing fine. Alicia stood away from us while my mom whispered in my ear.

What she said was that she had this intuition that my dad was going to show up somewhere on this tour. She could feel it in the weather and the landscape. She could still feel his anger in the air around us.

I said that I felt pretty certain my dad wouldn't be able to find us, and that if he did, he wasn't likely to hurt us. I told her not to worry. Right then I didn't have room in my feelings for anything but Larry.

All the while she was talking to me, I was watching Larry, who had stayed away from the spot where he and Brodie were supposed to stand, even though James had yammered at him to "move up into the light." Larry and Brodie kept standing to the side, quietly chatting, as if they were the only two men in the room, and they had just discovered some secret passion they held in common. Then I saw Mac glance over at Larry and nod that he was ready. Immediately, Larry touched Brodie's elbow, and the two of them moved into the lights.

They were transformed, in that they suddenly seemed larger than either one of them had appeared standing off to the side. But Larry was by far the most changed of the two of them. Whereas his face was ordinarily sort of closed, or at least subtle in what it conveyed, now it took on an animated quality. He was flashing this big smile that I hadn't seen before, but he also had a lifted eyebrow and a condescending look down his nose and a blink of surprise and about half a dozen other facial expressions that made you want to watch him every second. "That boy is very handsome, isn't he?" my mom whispered in my ear—we were still standing close to each other, and she still had her arm around my waist.

I knew she didn't mean anything racist by it, but I couldn't keep from pulling away from her and telling her, "Mom, I don't think you ought to be calling him a boy."

we went through the factory, and she was taking notes, but it was evident she had no taste for what she was doing. After she dutifully put her head inside this huge vat called a washback, she looked as if someone had just served her a horse turd for breakfast.

Later that afternoon, Mike pulled the bus up beside an old graveyard. On the other side of the road was what was left of an ancient stone church, or as Alicia informed us, the Ruin of Elgin Cathedral, founded in 1224 and burned to the ground in 1390 by the Wolf of Badenoch, whoever he was. James wanted shots of the Contemporary Black Man of the Year posing by this ruin.

It was late in the day. When we had stopped, there had been sunlight, but now there were dark thunderheads rolling in overhead and a frightening dimming of the daylight, as if we had suddenly entered an eclipse.

James must have been awfully determined to have his shot of Larry with one foot perched atop a slab of thirteenth century cathedral wall. James had produced a plaid cap for him to wear, but the wind was blowing so hard that to keep from losing it, Larry had to jam it down onto his head. Even Mac, who until now had seemed willing to indulge James in any whim, started yelling at James. Still James gestured at them, and they kept at it. Alicia, watching with Mike out of the driver's side window, shook her head and clucked her tongue at them.

When the raindrops did start pelting down, they were like rain in a cartoon, huge globs of water that hammered the bus roof and splatted on the windows. The first man back on the bus was James, stopping just inside the bus door to brush at his shoes with his handkerchief. Mac, just behind him, found James's rear end blocking his way into the bus, and yelled, "Move it, for Christ's sake, James!" James moved it, but over his shoulder, he spat back at Mac, "These are five hundred dollar shoes, baby!"

Larry was the last one on the bus and therefore got pretty wet. Before he sat down with me, Larry pulled off his wet sweater and hung it over the empty seat in front of us. I didn't try to talk with him, I just watched him fuming to himself and carefully blocking out the sweater on the bus seat. Though his white turtleneck fit him like a tank-top, I was surprised to see that it was worn almost threadbare. Suddenly I saw, not the successful New York male model with a huge personal wardrobe, but somebody struggling to survive by taking care of the few good clothes he owned. When Larry did sit down with me, he shook his fist behind the seat in the direction of James and whispered, "That son of a bitch!" I gave Larry what I hoped was a look that informed him I was ready to die for him.

With almost magical speed, Mike drove the bus out of Elgin and back up into the Highlands. All of a sudden we were riding out from under the rainstorm into a high, open sky. From up front, my mom looked back at me and caught my eye, gesturing with her head out to our left, as if she meant to make me the gift of the view out there. The sun shone on white clouds in the distance that floated like enormous zeppelins over a valley of farmers' fields; the clouds' shadows darkened patches of the green and brown countryside. There were stone walls by the road and snaking all down through the long gentle valley.

I've had years to think about this and compare it to other experiences I've had. In no circumstance have I ever felt as intensely connected to anyone as I did to Larry that day. I remember thinking that a gray-blue fringe on a rain-cloud was yellowish like an old woman's hair, and I knew that Larry saw it too and saw it just as I did. Two crows skimmed low over new-green fields in a patch of sunlight just beside the bus. I knew that I would never see anything more exquisite than that. I knew Larry saw it too and marked it to remember.

Just as we were coming into the driveway of the inn where we were staying, we both noticed, in the half-light of the field beside us, a black horse running through a field toward a barn and a gray horse walking that way, too. Those horses marked the end of our afternoon together and made it all right for us to go back into our separate lives.

Meldrun House, where we were staying, was a very fancy country inn. My mom and I were assigned to Room #1, which had a bed that was even bigger than king-sized, a fireplace, a huge bay window that looked out over a field toward a forest, and a bathroom in it as big as an ordinary hotel room.

My mom was quiet and sweet to me, drew me a bath, helped me wash my hair, and then blew it dry and brushed it for me, all the while asking me questions about Larry, speculating with me about him. She and I had a funny time of it dressing up for dinner—Alicia had told all of us that we should, and we'd been looking for an excuse to wear our fancy dresses. When we met for drinks, James had changed into another double-breasted suit and a raspberry-colored shirt with a white collar with a silk tie pinned up so that it puffed out of his jacket. Larry wore a navy tie with a tiny white polka dot in it that went perfectly with his navy blazer, white shirt, and gray flannel pants. He and I exchanged looks when we first saw each other, but without saying anything, we both understood that we weren't with each other that night.

That night I was with my mom almost as intensely as I had been with Larry until we got off the bus. The day had been one of clarity and sharp detail, but as I remember that evening now, everything seems as if it were being filmed in soft focus. The way I moved through the cocktail hour and the dinner felt like some pleasantly blurred dream I was having. Instead of drinking wine with the others, my mom drank ginger ale with me, as she had always done at our dinner parties at home. Where Larry and I had been wary of even brushing against each other, my mom and I were constantly touching. She would put her arm around my waist, I would lean my head on her shoulder, and one of us would catch the other's hand. Once she whispered to me, "Watch Mac flirting with Alicia," her lips brushing my ear in the most delicious way. I felt almost perverted enjoying the physical contact with my mom that way, though I knew it wasn't really sexual. Sexual was sitting with my shoulder three inches away from Larry's arm and feeling jolts of energy. Sexual was politely saying good-night to Larry after dinner and wanting to lie down on the floor and let him walk the length of my body on his way upstairs.

Not since I had been six or seven had I slept in the same bed with my mom, and the bed in Room #1 was so huge that we could have slept there with neither of us being aware of the other's presence. But my mom snuggled up to my back, and we stayed awake like that for a long time, talking and slipping into sleep, then talking a little more.

Next morning was sunny. On the bus, Larry and I sat to-gether again, with the difference in us mostly that now we felt released from yesterday's intensity enough to talk with each other. He was amused by what I told him about how his jazz tape had affected me; he said that I had been listening to Oscar Peterson and Dexter Gordon and that either of those guys would have laughed if they'd known how uptight I was listen-ing to them play.

The bus was climbing again, passing huge hillside fields with sheep spaced here and there in it as if they'd been directed to keep their distance from each other. Far ahead, we could see a snow-covered mountain. Even though we had come inland some miles now, there were still gulls flying the skies. Larry kept checking a map he had picked up at the airport. When I asked him why he seemed so interested in it, he told me that his grandmother was Scots–English and she'd lived in a little town he pointed out on the map. I hoped he didn't notice my blushing. Because he was black, I had assumed that all his relatives had to be black. His telling me about this Scotch–English grandmother made me suddenly understand that he was both black and white. Until that moment I think I had liked thinking of him as black and myself as white, the two of us different in some absolute way; it unsettled me to think of him as being the same as me—I had a Scotch–English grandmother, too—and then it embarrassed me that I was so shaken by something that I ought to have understood easily from the shade of his skin and his facial features, something that was really pretty ordinary when you thought about it.

I was quiet for too long. He must have known some of what I was thinking, because he grinned at me and told me he even had a Scottish name. "My real name's Hilary," he said. "Hilary Cooper," he said, as if it was important for me to hear the sound of his whole and proper name.

I was embarrassed over my assumptions and Larry's kindness toward me. He saw that. Another person might have patted my hand or something corny like that, and then I certainly would have cried, but Larry turned to the window, then whispered, "Look." There were three pheasants walking in a field like gaudy chickens. We were coming down a steep hill, alongside a rocky stream of dark water. Again it was as if Larry and I were seeing the world like two people singing harmony with each other. There were sheep in a plowed field, over which were crows, gulls, and clouds so white they seemed almost polished. There was a gull flying so far down in the valley that we were looking down on its gliding wings.

Later on, James made us stop by one of those steep hillside pastures to try to get pictures of the Contemporary Black Man of the Year standing beside a sheep. Even though there was a cold wind out there, James wanted Larry to be wearing only his T-shirt. The sheep wouldn't cooperate, so that James had Larry and Mac running over that hillside in pursuit of a sheep. From the bus, the chasing looked silly and fun, but when they gave up and came back, Larry was cold and furious. He sat down, rubbing his arms and whispering, "That son of a bitch, that son of a bitch."

I figured out that in my company Larry was able to release some of his anxieties and to be himself in a way that he usually wasn't. I even understood that he was at ease around me because he thought I was a kid who wasn't any threat to him.

But aside from my dad, Larry was the most ambitious person I'd ever met. Like me, he was an only child. His dad was a personnel manager for Dupont, his mom was a social worker, and they read books and went to concerts and museums and discussed current events at dinner. All through high school and college, his friends and acquaintances had been saying stuff to him like "Yo, brother, what's happening?" and treating him like somebody who'd grown up in the ghetto. Larry laughed about it when he told me, but anybody would have known it wasn't funny to him. "I was putting on that phony Black English the same as all the white kids," he said. He was embarrassed to bring his friends home with him because his home-life was so ordinary. When I asked him how he got started modeling, he shaded his eyes with his hand and said, "I like clothes, Angela. I like nice clothes." Then he went on to say that if he'd known he would have to put up with people like James, he'd have definitely tried some other career.

Way up in the highlands we saw these little stone houses that we thought had been abandoned; we talked about how hard the lives of the people who lived there must have been. Larry said he'd give anything to be able to go inside one of those places. When I suggested that Alicia and Mike probably wouldn't mind stopping, Larry chuckled and said, "All we'd need would be for James to get it in his mind to have some shots of me posing in front of one of those places."

Once while Larry was sleeping, I noticed a hawk cruising in the air right along with the bus. Then it turned toward us and seemed to be coming straight at us, belly-forward. For an instant it was just at my window; then we were past it, and I was sitting there with my heart beating, and no one else on the bus had noticed it.

Another time—and this was just at dusk when we were way up in the mountains—two jet fighters roared up over the horizon and over our bus, sounding like the end of the world. Larry shook his head as if he couldn't believe what he'd seen and heard, or didn't want to believe it. Except for the highway, the landscape was prehistoric—a couple of dinosaurs would have been more believable.

So it wasn't like everything I saw was pure beauty. The more days that went by and the more distilleries we had to plod through, the darker my mom's mood became. As I remember it now, I think that each time we stepped into one of those buildings, without admitting it to each other, we both started thinking about my dad's drinking and worrying about what he might do. Now when she and I slept together in a hotel room,

I was the one who curled around her back and woke her up and told her it was all right when she started whimpering in her sleep. I wondered if my dad usually woke her up or let her sleep through her nightmares.

In Edinburgh, our schedule gave us the morning to do whatever we wanted to do. After breakfast in the Sheraton dining room, my mom and I decided to go for a walk in the park below Edinburgh Castle. While we stood outside the hotel entrance, blinking in the sunlight and trying to get our bearings, Larry came out, looking like a Moroccan prince in his long gray overcoat, and said good morning to us. I spoke to him in my usual floaty way, because I'd gotten used to being distant from him when we weren't on the bus. It wasn't anything we'd decided to do; we'd never talked about why we did things that way. If Larry had thought about it, he'd probably decided that it would be asking for trouble for a twenty-four-year-old black man to be hanging out with a thirteen-year-old white girl. If I'd thought about it, I'd have known that, too, but I'm not sure either of us really put our minds to it. It was just there, in both our consciousnesses, but whenever we saw each other accidentally like that, we each had this special grin for communicating to the other, "Hey, I'll see you on the bus."

Until now, my mom had taken on a kind of warm but distant way of speaking to Larry, as if she meant to convey to him an understanding about how I was to be treated. This morning, though, she seemed really happy to see him and invited him to go with us on our walk.

It was easy finding our way down into the park, which was named the West Princess Street Gardens and which was filled with beds of blooming daffodils, tulips, and hyacinths. The day was sunny and sort of half warm, but there was a little stream of running water down there, and then there was a huge cliff on top of which loomed Edinburgh Castle. The cliff and the castle generated darkness and cold air.

My mom took Larry's arm. Though it seemed almost a violation of our rules, when he offered me his other one, I took it. While we strolled slowly along the paths, my mom told Larry everything about why we were on the tour and about my dad maybe trying to track us down and about Michael Land hoping to work out some kind of agreement before we got back to London. I didn't know why she was telling him all that, but then she stopped walking, made us all three stand there in the middle of the park and made Larry promise that if anything happened to her, he would help me get back in touch with Michael Land in London. I don't know why I wasn't more embarrassed by her.

She gave Larry Michael Land's card and thanked him and kissed him on the cheek. That did embarrass me, and him, too. Then she said she wanted to go back to the Sheraton, but if the two of us wanted to stay out a while longer, it was all right with her. Larry and I exchanged just a glance, but that was enough for me to understand that he didn't want to be out there alone with me, and so I said I felt like going back to the Sheraton, too. Larry said he thought he might have time for a quick visit to the Sir Walter Scott Monument down at the far end of the park.

Walking back through the West Princess Street Gardens, my mom and I linked arms, and laughed about how uncurious we were to visit Edinburgh Castle up there above us. We laughed about it looking like a monster's forehead peeping over the edge of the cliff. My mom was at a time in her life when it seemed possible for her to be four or five different ages. Right then, giggling with me about the dumb castle, she seemed no more than twenty-five, but a few minutes earlier, telling Larry about her "estrangement" from my dad, she had had that sad, weary slumping of the shoulders that you see in women well over fifty.

When we walked into the lobby of the Sheraton, James trotted up to us and asked if we'd seen Larry. My mom said she thought Larry was doing some sightseeing. James's eyes got very hard, and he said, "I'm going to have to kill that boy," speaking directly to me. Then he gave this very forced laugh and turned his back on us.

Around noon we packed up the bus and loaded up, all of us acting tired and cranky. Mike got lost looking for the place where we were to have lunch. Mac had a Barbra Streisand tape that he insisted on putting on the bus's sound system with the volume cranked up. I couldn't tell if he thought it was a treat for us or if he simply meant it as an assault on those of us who had no use for Streisand, which would have been most notably Larry and me. James, who until then had been very decent about not smoking on the bus, decided to light up because, as he explained it, he never listened to Streisand without having a cigarette. Everyone on the bus got very quiet except for Mac and James who shouted at each other about the music, about how much they loved this song and how good Streisand was in such and such a movie and how such and such a singer was trying to imitate her. Larry had been silently furious, but all of a sudden he started chuckling. "Doesn't that say it all? Fucking Streisand." It was funny, but I understood that that was just about the worst thing Larry would ever say about somebody.

If he had been slow getting us to lunch in Edinburgh, Mike made up for lost time driving us to Glasgow. I slept for what seemed like only a few minutes; when I woke up we were in the city. For a moment I wondered if we'd even left Edinburgh, but it took only another moment or so before I saw how different everything looked, a city with darker colors and a much denser texture. Larry told me our first stop was to be a Glasgow pub.

Exhaustion was catching up with me. I couldn't seem to wake up while Mike was maneuvering the bus through the narrow city streets. Glasgow was like this dream I was having, as if I were floating into a painting of a city with rows of dark-colored buildings and sidewalks crowded with these fast-walking, light-skinned people in dark clothes. I had no desire to do anything; the idea of going into a pub seemed silly to me. When Mike found a parking space, I told Larry I wanted to stay on the bus and take a nap. He told me he thought I ought to make the effort. He nodded up toward the front, where I saw my mom looking back at me, smiling but obviously worried about something.

Michton's Tavern it was called. It was noisy, crowded, and almost bizarrely cheerful, as if everyone in there were being paid to put on a smile and to shout in a jovial voice. It would have been smoky, too, except that the huge room had such a high ceiling that all the smoke rose and lingered twenty feet above our heads. Behind the bar, a wall of bottles rose so high that they must have used ladders to fetch the ones on the last two or three shelves. Back there was an enormous mirror tilted so that the crowd of us could look up over the bar into it and see this weirdly suspended reflection of ourselves.

The customers were mostly businessmen in suits and smartly dressed women. A man nudged another man and nodded toward Larry; they and their lady friends looked him over greedily as if he were somebody famous.

I found myself looking into the pale blue eyes of a tall and excessively handsome bartender who seemed most amused by my spaciness. My mom and I were standing together near the busy end of the bar. I must have been staring all around me with my mouth wide open. "What can I get for you, Miss?" he asked.

Before I could say anything, a waitress came up beside us and told the bartender, "I've got it right here, Ritchie." She handed him a note, and he turned to fill the order. I didn't think anything about it; it was a busy place; it didn't seem odd for a waitress to interrupt a bartender's waiting on an American tourist who'd obviously take a while before she decided what she wanted to order. But suddenly the waitress was handing drinks to us, tall glasses of ginger ale for my mom and me.

In that noisy, relentlessly cheerful crowd of drinking Scots, my mom and I accepted the glasses, surprised and pleased that someone would have treated us, that someone would have known what drinks we'd have been likely to order. Then we began realizing who would have known what we'd want to drink. My mom turned pale; then she and I started looking around for him.

The waitress stood watching us, brightly smiling, certain we would be delighted with the surprise she had delivered to us. Looking into her half-pretty face, I had this eerie glimpse of her life: she had lots of brothers and sisters and a boyfriend who worked there at Michton's behind the bar on a different shift. The two of them had just moved into an apartment a couple of blocks away. She was a regular-looking girl, with clean hair and a small waist; she had all this energy in her, all this life. She pointed toward a table in the back corner of the room. My dad was sitting there, leaning around people so that we could see him.

For a second I thought my mom might faint. Her eyes widened; she flinched. But then I saw her jaw tighten. She touched my arm. "Let's go say hello to your father," she murmured. As we started through the crowd, she touched Larry on the sleeve but kept moving. When Larry caught my eye he seemed to read the whole story. He had been talking with Alicia and Mike; I heard him say, "Excuse me," and I knew he was following along behind us.

My dad was smiling widely. I was surprised that he wasn't at least standing up to greet us. He had on a dark green jacket, a striped tie, and a white shirt that looked so fresh he might have just put it on. Even in that crowd of well-dressed people, my dad seemed the most dressed up of all. His hair was perfectly trimmed, he had a light suntan, and his teeth gleamed. There was a coffee cup on the table in front of him, which meant he was sober. He nodded at my mom and said, "Kathleen," in his voice that said he hated her and he loved her all at the same time. He reached up toward me, so that I knew I was supposed to give him a hug. His shoulders and neck and head felt strange to me, so stiff and rigid that he must have been very keyed up for this meeting. The only thing familiar about him was the cologne I'd known to be his for as long as I could remember. He smelled as if he'd showered and shaved no more than an hour ago.

When I stepped back from him, I saw him looking quizzically up at Larry who stood behind my mom. "Dad, this is Larry," I told him. "Larry, this is my dad." Larry stepped forward and leaned down to shake my dad's hand. Neither of them said a word; they actually grimaced at each other, as if acknowledging that they'd have preferred not to have to go through this introduction. Then Larry stepped back behind my mom.

My dad put his grin back on his face, looking at me and then my mom, who was making herself meet his eyes. "My little family," he said and shook his head. "You sure are hard to track down when you take a vacation." Like his pleasant expression, his voice had an easy sound to it, but I knew that my mom was hearing in it what I was, that edge of meanness. He pushed his coffee cup forward and folded his hands on the table in front of him, so that his pressed white cuffs and tanned hands and manicured nails were an exhibit for us to view. "Kathleen," he said, and this time there was a change in the pitch of his voice; the meanness was gone, but it was scarier without it. "Kathleen, for half my life, I've known exactly where you were almost every hour of the day."

My mom inhaled and held her breath, but my dad raised his left hand as if to stop her from speaking. "I'm not here to be petty," he said, looking her in the eye for just a moment, then quickly flicking a look at me.

"Kathleen," he said, dipping his head and bringing his eyes back to my mom's face again. I saw Larry studying him, squinting at him as if my dad were a professor explaining how to solve some very difficult problem. "Kathleen, you know I'm not a moderate person."

"Yes," my mom said so softly I could barely hear her. She stepped forward to set her purse on his table and folded her arms. "Yes, Frank," she said, and now her normal voice had come back to her. "I know what kind of a person you are." My mom was wearing ordinary slacks and a sweater and a tweed jacket, but she was standing as if she meant for her body to tell my dad that she wasn't afraid of him. Their eyes were locked.

My dad's mouth twitched for a moment I couldn't tell if he was sneering or grinning at her. Then he dug into his jacket pocket and came up with a ring of keys which he tossed onto the table beside her purse. "Those are my keys to your car and to the house. You don't have to change the locks," he said. "All my stuff is out. By the time you get back to London, my lawyer should have worked out an agreement with Michael."

My mom kept standing still and looking at him, but her body seemed to soften its attitude. My dad, too, kept looking at her and not moving. The tension seemed to leave them while I watched. Finally my mom picked up those keys and her purse and said, "Thank you." My dad closed his eyes and nodded his head ever so slightly.

When she turned away from the table, he stood up to give me a hug. This time when I pressed against him, he really did seem himself. I kissed his cheek and told him, "Thanks," though I couldn't imagine what I was thanking him for.

"You take care, baby girl," he said.

When I turned away from him, I expected Larry to be there waiting for me, and he was. He didn't touch me, but he stayed right beside me while we walked out of that place. We found my mom, looking lost out in the afternoon light. While I took her in my arms and patted her back, Larry stood there with us, looking fiercely up and down the sidewalk.

That night, at the old Glasgow Hotel where we were staying, there was an extravagant farewell dinner, at which Larry and James appeared, arm in arm and decked out in kilts and formal jackets with black ties and studded white shirts. I remember that, even as miserable as I felt that night, I recognized how Larry had performed some sort of magic trick in looking as if he were born to those red-and-black-plaid clothes of a chieftain, those tasseled knee socks and silver-buckled patent leather shoes.

But then watching him and James acting like such cozy pals made me feel sick in my heart. My mom, in her blue silk cocktail dress, was so radiant that James, who had paid almost no attention to her for the whole tour, now pulled Larry over with him to talk to her. The three of them started laughing, James leaning back to guffaw, holding onto Larry's shoulder to keep his balance.

This is the part that makes my eyes sting each time I remember it. All of a sudden I was furious at James. Even though I was standing right beside Alicia, I rasped out, "Damn him!" Alicia gave me this horrified look, and I heard my voice firing again, "That son of a bitch!" Then I started crying.

When I came out from the ladies' room, having calmed myself down but not having had much luck fixing my weepy face, they were all there waiting for me. "Larry wants you to have your picture taken with him," my mom told me. She was too caught up in being happy even to see me. I heard Larry right beside me saying, "Come on, Angela."

In his voice, I imagined that I heard everything: gulls and pheasants we'd seen in the fields, the hawk soaring off down through the dark valley, the insane jet fighters roaring up over the mountains, the black horse running and the gray horse walking toward the barn across the deep green field at dusk. I imagined that his voice was telling me how he would hold in his memory those things the two of us had seen and that those days we had spent together riding through Scotland would be a part of his life forever. Walking with him over to the huge fireplace of the hotel dining room, I stopped looking at Hilary Cooper in his costume. When we turned to face Mac with his cameras and all the others laughing and cheering behind the blinding lights, I knew what those pictures were going to look like: there would be this smiling young black man in Scottish regalia with his arm around a gangly-limbed adolescent girl with a puffy face and scraped eyes. I didn't care about any of that. I knew I wouldn't ever have to look at the silly picture. I looked into the light and smiled as if I were even happier than my mom.

Henry Lagoon

To TEASE HIM, kids in his sixth grade started calling him "Lagoon." And because of something his father had once said, Henry thought a goon was a large and formidable man. The name held a certain power, and he liked it, but he pretended he didn't so that they'd keep on with it. By ninth grade his classmates had almost forgotten his real name was Lague.

In 1930 Henry's grandfather, Laurent Lague, had come down from Quebec City to Barre, Vermont, to work in the granite quarry. When he was Henry's age, Henry's father, Philip Lague, had also gone to work for Rock of Ages and spent most of his lifetime engineering room-sized blocks of stone up out of the earth for a foreman's wages.

Henry had just become aware that he didn't know what he was to become. He knew he wasn't poor or rich, ugly or good-looking, smart or stupid, tall, short, fat, thin, fast or slow. He thought himself to be a profoundly unremarkable fourteen-year-old boy with brown hair, a kid who didn't hold anybody's interest.

"Bedroom eyes," Patty Boulanger told him some of the girls had decided he had. Henry didn't know what that meant; he was insulted until Patty assured him. "It's like—," she said and she hooded her eyes and let her lips go kind of loose.

"Oh," Henry said, but he didn't understand.

All of a sudden Henry found that he had himself a girlfriend, not Patty Boulanger, who'd merely been a messenger, but Lisa Yancey, a freshman of some consequence because she'd just had her braces off, and it turned out she had a smile that before she got it under control had the senior boys asking her out for dates. Lisa Yancey was probably the only girl at Spaulding High School who thought Henry had bedroom eyes or who even thought at all about Henry. A couple of days after that bedroom-eyes conversation, she and Patty had fallen in beside him walking home from school. They'd gone into Frank's for a soda. At the booth where they ended up, Lisa moved over for Henry to sit beside her. When Henry got his nerve up enough to glance over at her, she looked back at him, and neither one of them looked away until she gave him almost a full smile and he blushed.

Now every day after school they stopped off at Frank's for a soda and for Lisa to ask Henry his opinions of the people they knew at school. Usually he said something like, "He's OK" or "She's kind of cute," after which Lisa told him what she thought of that person. Her opinions were complex and fascinating; Henry thought it was amazing that she thought so much about these people. One day, at the corner where they always stopped before she walked up the street toward her house, Lisa told him she thought his wrong name ought to be his right one. "I think you ought to change it." She laughed as she said that, but he didn't take it as a joke.

Henry hadn't considered what she'd think of either his wrong or his right name. But he decided it was OK for her to be the one who decided once and for all about his name. He watched her walk up that way under the bare trees. It was a November day and sunny but chilly. Lisa had on a cream-colored fisherman's sweater, a long black skirt, knee socks to match her sweater, and small red shoes. The sun shone on her black hair. Shifting her book bag to her other shoulder, she turned enough to notice Henry standing there watching her walk up the hill. She waved, and he waved back. Then the two of them stood there with seventy-five yards of sidewalk between them, just looking at each other. Henry felt his blood rocketing through his veins.

After school on a Friday afternoon, he persuaded Lisa to hitch with him over to the state offices in Montpelier to find out how he could legally change his name. A lady behind a counter told him that without his parents' signature, he couldn't do it until he was eighteen. This was a pudgy, dressed-up lady with a permanent and tinted glasses. "You can take these forms, if you want to, honey, but if I were your mother, I wouldn't sign." She pushed the papers over the counter toward him and shook her head. Before he took them, Henry glanced over at Lisa, who looked scared and thin under the fluorescent lights. He brushed her hand to turn her toward the door. Neither of them thanked the lady.

Outside, even though it was not much above freezing, Henry and Lisa sat down on the bench in front of the FM radio station. He started filling out the forms.

"God, this is peculiar," Lisa said. She was wearing jeans and a bright red parka over a pink sweater.

"It might be," Henry said solemnly. He knew he wouldn't be filling out these forms—wouldn't even have made this trip—if it weren't for Lisa. On the other hand, maybe this wasn't what she had in mind. She might be deciding that this was so strange that it would be the last thing she'd ever do with him. He signed his name at the bottom of the forms and stared at the blank lines where he knew his parents would never put their signatures. He couldn't even see himself showing them these forms. After a while he folded up the papers and put them in his shirt pocket inside his jacket.

His and Lisa's relationship was chaste. Inside Frank's they usually sat so close to each other that their shoulders and their arms touched, but that was it so far. Hitching over to Montpelier, Henry had put his arm around her when they both climbed into a pick-up truck that'd stopped for them. Lisa had snuggled in close, but Henry thought that was because she didn't like the scruffy old guy who was driving.

Now she surprised him by reaching over and patting his jacket where the forms were. It seemed to him an intimate thing to do. Henry studied her greenish brown eyes. Her expression was serious.

"Hey, Lisa," he said, very softly because their faces were so close together.

"What?" She spoke just as softly as he had.

He shook his head and looked down and smiled. "Lagoon is going to have to wait," he said.

"Lagoon," Lisa said, smiling to herself as if the word were one she liked. Her voice made Henry see a tropical beach with palm trees and white sand.

They had no trouble getting a ride back to Barre, this time in a station wagon driven by a lady with a sleeping baby in a car seat and six bags of groceries in the back. Henry got in front with the woman, Lisa in back with the baby. Henry thought the woman looked familiar, but she didn't ask him any questions, just let them out at Frank's when he asked her to.

Out on the sidewalk with nobody around them, Henry waited to see what Lisa would say. He stretched and grinned at her, as if he'd been sleeping and had just now waked up. She didn't look scared any more; she looked like she didn't care who drove by and saw them standing together. He thought he was beginning to catch on to Lisa.

"Henry Lagoon," she said, "do you want to come over to my house and make a video?" The look she gave him now was not so much a smile as it was an expression of openness. It scared him that she let him see how much this mattered to her.

"I'll have to call my mom," he told her. They went into Frank's where he used the pay phone while she went to the ladies' room. He knew his mother would ask a lot of dumb questions. Right off she wanted to know whose house he was going to. When he told her Lisa Yancey's, his mother paused a moment and then spoke to him in a different voice. She said she knew Lisa's mom and dad and to call her if he was going to be later than six-thirty getting home. Then she told him to have a nice time and said goodbye. Henry had expected her to put up more resistance. When he turned around and his eyes met Lisa's, he knew he had a stupid grin on his face.

So they walked up Valliere Street to the Yanceys' house. Henry guessed he'd seen it before; it was a white clapboard, three-story house with green shutters and a skylight in the roof. Lisa led him up the driveway, past neatly mulched-down flower beds, and around to the back porch. Before he was quite ready for it, he was inside the quiet house.

"Come on," Lisa told him, leading him into the carpeted hallway and up the carpeted steps. Taking off her parka as she padded up the steps, she seemed deeply purposeful, attentive only to the fact of Henry's following her. She dropped the red jacket on the floor at the top of the stairs, then paused a moment. Her sweater was pink with a marbled pattern around the collar. There was a window up there that framed her with the silky light of a late November afternoon. Henry stopped climbing a couple of steps from the top and watched her slip off one loafer and then the other. Lisa's jeans and sweater weren't at all tight—they weren't the kind of clothes that invited people to look at you—but Henry studied her carefully. She stood still, something out that window having caught her eye. He could see her as much as he wanted to.

"Come on," she finally said, turning to him. Now she had another kind of look for him. The rest of the steps disappeared beneath his feet; he was instantly there and following her.

She led him down the hallway and turned left to a door that opened into a large room with bright yellow walls, yellow carpet, white curtains, and a white bedspread. Sunlight beamed through the windows. Henry shivered with the sensation of standing beside Lisa on the threshold of that room full of light. "My mom and dad's room," she told him. The objects on top of the two dressers were arranged in patterns that Henry knew would be instantly apparent if disturbed. "My dad makes the bed and straightens up every morning," Lisa said. Henry nodded. They stood a moment or two longer before she turned and led him away from her parents' bedroom.

The room across the hall, Henry knew, had to be Lisa's. When she opened the door and he saw inside, he was glad the room wasn't weird. There was a four-poster bed with a pink canopy over it; the covers had been pulled up over the sheets, but the bed wasn't really made up. There was a shelf of books with dolls and stuffed animals on top of it. There was a desk with a jar of pencils and a lamp on it. There was a dresser with a jewelry box, a piggy bank, and a scattering of pins and ribbons. Under the window was a large, new-looking metal case.

Lisa sat down in the chair at her desk. Henry leaned against the foot of the bed. Lisa studied him as if deciding whether or not to trust him. Then she knelt by the metal case and opened it. It was a new Magnavox video recorder with an elaborate audio recording component and some basic lighting equipment. She began unpacking in a way that Henry recognized as much-practiced.

Henry thought that she was taking pleasure in what she was doing, that she was demonstrating something. She set up three lights on stands. She mounted the video recorder on a tripod. She unwound wire from a microphone and connected it to a boxy component she set up on her desk. Handing the microphone to Henry, she plugged everything into a board of electrical outlets, apparently newly installed at the baseboard beside her desk. She stood up and sighted through the recorder's peephole in Henry's general direction.

"We're almost ready," she said. She snapped on the lights she'd set up, then readjusted the tripod, raising the camera to point over Henry's shoulder.

While she worked, Henry watched how her dark hair swung this way and that. From the side of the case she plucked a small remote control unit. Their eyes met for one moment when she reached to take the microphone from him. Then she walked to the side of the bed, brushing a strand of hair away from her eyes. "Come down here, please, Henry." He did what she said. She sat down and swung herself over to the other side, plumping up the pillow behind her so that she was at least partially sitting up and facing the video recorder. When she motioned for him to join her, Henry stumbled, unlaced his boots and took them off, then uneasily arranged himself on the bed beside her. He hoped he'd remembered to put on clean socks that morning. From the window sill Lisa pulled over a stuffed Kermit the Frog, fixed the microphone in its arms, then set it between them. Pointing the remote at the camera, she switched the thing on. It whirred in silence with its red light eying them. "Go ahead," Lisa whispered. Henry was aware of her watching him.

He cleared his throat. "My name is Henry Lagoon," he told the camera. "L-a-g-o-o-n. I'm a freshman at Spaulding High School. I study fairly hard, but my grades aren't that great. I might get a paper route in a couple of weeks." He paused, then turned to Lisa and said, "Your turn."

Lisa blinked as if she wasn't ready. Henry was thrilled when he saw that she was blushing. She ducked her head and began speaking. "My name is Lisa Yancey. I'm a freshman at Spaulding High School. Henry and I just got back from hitch-hiking to Montpelier. I'd never done that before."

"I hadn't either," Henry added.

"Henry is changing his name," Lisa explained to the video recorder. "To Lagoon. It's what everybody calls him anyway. He and I like it. It makes me think of this lake up in Canada where there isn't anything but these huge hemlock trees and water that's clear and still as a mirror. Anyway, Patty Boulanger introduced us about two weeks ago, and this is the first time Henry has ever been to my house."

"Patty thinks I have bedroom eyes," Henry put in almost absentmindedly. He was still thinking about Lisa's lake in Canada.

"But you don't," Lisa said.

Momentarily Henry was stopped in his thoughts. Then he saw Lisa grinning at him. "Do," Henry said, as if he were idly quarreling with his sister. He made a vague gesture around the room, as if to suggest the room itself to be evidence of his bedroom eyes. Then he sat up, crossed his legs, put his hands on his knees, looked directly at the camera, and imitated the loose-lipped look Patty Boulanger had shown him to demonstrate bedroom eyes. Wondering what was keeping her silent, he suddenly became aware of Lisa behind him with forked fingers raised over his head. There was one thing to do: tickle her. She turned out to be most rewardingly ticklish. The bed squeaked and squawked with them rolling around on it like that.

"You're going to break the microphone!" she shrieked at him just when he was about to pin her hands with one of his hands so that he could tickle her good with the other one.

He stopped. They both looked at the place where Kermit and the microphone were supposed to be but weren't any longer. Henry let her go. He pretended it was because he had to pick up the name-changing forms that'd fallen out of his pocket over onto the edge of the bed. Lisa plunged her hands down into the crack between the headboard and the mattress and came up with the frog and the dangling microphone, holding them up like a rescued baby and its pacifier. The look she gave him articulated what Henry was thinking as clearly as if she'd said it aloud. He simply bent forward and directed his lips toward hers. Lisa bent her head slightly this way; Henry bent his that way.

"Lisa!" The two syllables came directly down from the ceiling above the bed's canopy. Between the shock of hearing that voice and the soft trance of kissing Lisa, Henry was paralyzed.

"Yes, daddy?" Lisa called.

"What are you doing?"

"We're making a video." Lisa put her hands on Henry's shoulders and grinned at him, even while she answered her father.

"Who's making a video?"

"Henry and I are."

"Henry who?"

"Henry Lagoon."

There was a long pause before the voice sounded again. Finally it sent down a decree: "You and Henry Lague go downstairs and have something to eat."

"OK, daddy." The two of them maneuvered themselves and the microphone off the bed.

The voice boomed once more: "Henry, tell your mom and dad I said hello."

"Yes, sir," squeaked Henry. His face was burning.

Lisa extracted the cassette and turned off the recorder. She turned off the lights and dismantled the light stands. When he finished lacing his boots, Henry awkwardly helped her put all the equipment back in its case.

Lisa carried the cassette downstairs with her. At the top of the stairs, she ignored her jacket on the floor, but Henry picked up his before he followed her down. In the kitchen, Lisa explained it to him. Her dad kept a studio in the attic; a graphics designer for Rock of Ages, he worked at home. She showed Henry a small bulletin board by the telephone where somebody had thumbtacked several black-and-white photographs of gravestones. "These are my dad's latest," she said, tapping a granite angel with a finger lifted toward heaven. There was also a fat, flower-embellished cross, and there was even a granite dolphin plunging up out of the grassy surface of a graveyard. Henry didn't want to see these things. He turned back toward Lisa.

"But why did he stay quiet all that time before he said anything?"

"I don't know," Lisa said. She seemed to be puzzling through the question.

Henry stared at her. "Did you know he was up there?" he asked.

Lisa nodded. "He's almost always up there." Her expression was one of amusement, as if her father's behavior were something she'd just now considered.

For a moment Lisa's life opened up in Henry's mind. He was able to see Lisa coming home from school by herself and the house being quiet because her mom wasn't there and Lisa's getting a coke and some crackers to take upstairs to her room and climbing the carpeted stairs stopping to call, "Hi, Daddy," up the stairwell to the third floor. He could see Lisa going into her room, setting her food on her desk and her backpack on the floor, then kneeling down beside the case of video recording equipment and opening it. He could see Patty Boulanger coming home with Lisa and the two of them setting up the equipment to record Patty's version of bedroom eyes. No matter how much horsing around they'd do, Mr. Yancey wouldn't call down to them. He'd probably enjoy hearing them laughing with each other.

"How does your dad know my mom and dad?"

"He knows everybody in Barre from a long time ago." She shrugged. "And I told him some things about you. Do you want to watch the tape?" She was leaning against the kitchen counter, and she held the cassette in front of her and shook it, as if to tempt Henry with something she knew he craved.

Henry liked how Lisa was looking at him and liked her teasing tone of voice, but right then his feelings were absolutely known to him. He shook his head at her because he had no desire to see the two of them on TV wrestling around and tickling each other. Most definitely he didn't want to watch that kiss. Maybe it'd have been different if he hadn't found out that her father was in the house listening to them. He took a step toward her.

Lisa set the cassette on the counter. "Yes?" she said, slightly bending her head.

Even after they said goodbye, Lisa stood on her back porch, hugging herself to keep warm and watching him while he tried to look natural sidestepping away from her. At a certain distance, Henry caught this glimpse of Lisa exactly as she would look when she was as old as his mom. A surge of affection rose in him for the way she was going to be.

Walking home in the chilly November twilight, Henry thought about that second kiss, how it was something he and Lisa had chosen instead of something that just happened to them accidentally and how it went on until they stopped of their own accord, not because her father had called out her name. "Yes?" Lisa had said it like a question, just as her eyes closed.

He kicked leaves off the sidewalk of Valliere Street and swore he was going to leave Barre when he graduated. He had lots of time to decide where he'd go. Lisa's idea about the lake in Canada and all those trees wasn't the same as his about the tropical beach and the ocean, but they were both another place. In that pale light Henry couldn't make out much of his future, but he thought he could see some of its most interesting parts. He patted his jacket and felt the papers still there in his shirt pocket. He'd throw them away the first chance he got.

Little Sawtooth

MY LIVING ROOM is twelve feet wide and twenty-five feet long; it feels both large and cozy. I work there in the hours just before and after dawn, the hours when my wife and daughters sleep most deeply in the bedrooms upstairs. Since my laptop computer screen is lighted, I don't have to turn on any lamps. I write while sitting on the sofa with the fireplace opposite me and the empty wing chairs facing me as if they held ghosts whose duty is to watch me struggle with my early morning compositions.

More and more, my writing has caused me to examine my past—or maybe more accurately, my past has begun to examine *me*. Surprising things have come back to me for no discernible reason.

Someone I knew at the University of Idaho twenty-two years ago has been paying me some memory calls this past month. She's a woman I knew from what was a particularly harsh period for me, the beginning of my separation from my first wife. I was finding living alone almost unbearable, but I was afflicted with Recent Divorcé's Syndrome, the symptoms of which are simultaneous desire and hostility. It's a good thing I'd enrolled in graduate school, because anything more structured than that would have had me committing crimes of violence.

Michelle Gonyaw was the young woman with whom I fell into acquaintanceship. She, too—though it took me a while to see it—was a case-study in pain that year. I of course thought I was the only human being on the planet who'd ever been so severely singed by love. After our Whitman-and-Crane seminar was over each Tuesday and Thursday afternoon, I'd catch up with Michelle and chat with her while we walked toward town. Actually I was doing most of the talking and most of it about myself, but of course that's not what I thought I was doing. And she wasn't friendly either, which is probably why I persisted.

A few years younger than I was, Michelle dressed in the plainest, darkest, loosest clothes she could find and kept her black hair cut short. She tried to make herself invisible, but people noticed her anyway—I did at the very first meeting of our seminar. She couldn't hide her big violet eyes and her skin that was the lightest I've ever seen on a healthy person. At the time I took pride in not being sexually attracted to her—I just thought she was odd and probably an outcast like me—but my guess now is that her way of presenting herself allowed me to be sexually attracted to her without my realizing it.

"You know you dress like a god-damn nun," I told her one afternoon, walking toward town. That was the tone I used with her most of the time.

She snorted, the first time she'd shown any sign of being amused by me. "Yes," she said. "That's exactly what I am, a god-damn—a god-*damned* nun."

let me think about what she'd told me. It took quite a few nights to get the whole story out of her.

From Spirit Lake, north of Coeur d'Alene, where she'd grown up, Michelle had gone to college down in Boise. She wanted to be a teacher. She had what she thought of as a standard liberal arts education until her senior year when she signed up to take English history from a new instructor, just out of graduate school at the University of North Carolina. He had all these fancy fellowships—and had even studied at Cambridge University in England—but Professor Hammett Wilson had never taught any classes before he showed up for his first one at Boise State.

He spoke about English history the way revivalist preachers talk about Jesus, except that instead of repeating everything three or four times and shouting and carrying on, Hammett Wilson was brilliantly articulate. Michelle said he'd be broken out in a sweat, pacing the floor and gesturing, but he'd be speaking with this incredible lucidity and precision.

According to Michelle, he wasn't anything special to look at, a man of medium height and build, average taste in clothes, brown eyes, brown hair that fell over his forehead, and glasses, which he wore all the time, except when he lectured. Michelle said you could almost hear the whole class exhaling when Hammett Wilson set all his books and notes down on the desk, stood up straight, smiled at them, and took off his glasses.

What happened between Hammett Wilson and Michelle Gonyaw was that one morning when he took his glasses off to begin lecturing, he was looking straight into Michelle's eyes. He seemed to want to look away but to be unable to manage it for a long moment. For the rest of the class Michelle felt paralyzed. Hammett took up the lecture in his normal manner, except that again and again his eyes came back to Michelle's. At the end of class, he walked over to her desk to ask her to stop by his office that afternoon. He hadn't even learned her name, so that he had to ask her that: "Sometime after two o'clock, Miss—?"

Michelle said she knew she shouldn't have gone, but she had no more choice about it than she did about taking her next breath. She knew Hammett was married. He was the kind of man who, even though he'd been in town only a couple of months, had taken his wife and two young boys with him to everything on campus that might be of interest to a new teacher. Michelle had been raised a Catholic. She said that in the student union snack bar she sat alone like a hypnotized person until two o'clock. When she stood up to walk over to Hammett's office, she knew her old life was over.

His door was open, but she knocked anyway, standing just inside the threshold. He'd been looking out the window with his back to the door. When she heard her, he stood up and turned. They stayed like that a moment or two, until he finally stepped around behind her to close the door. Michelle wouldn't spell it out for me, but I gather that he let his hand brush across her shoulders when he turned back from the closed door.

"What he mostly did was whisper—because the walls of his office were so thin," she said. "But it was very intense whispering. He liked to have long talks like that, the two of us standing there holding each other, whispering with our mouths almost touching each other's ears." Michelle said she thought it was strange, but she didn't mind it.

She also said, "I was the one of us who was more physically aggressive," meaning me to understand, I think, that she wasn't some innocent country girl who had let herself be seduced.

But I think nothing much more than whispering, kissing, and maybe a little touching happened in that office. How many times she visited him there is not clear to me, but I doubt if it was very many. No one suspected them of anything. It was still early enough in the fall for them to think about taking a drive out Sunset Peak Road toward the National Forest.

Having been a member of the Outing Club since her freshman year, Michelle had come to know that mountainous countryside between Boise and Sun Valley. About fifty miles out of Boise, there was a place called Little Sawtooth Falls that she wanted Hammett to see. Michelle considered it her own private park. She had the idea they could talk there in their normal voices.

That second week of October Hammett's wife had taken their two boys to visit her sister in Portland. When Hammett told Michelle that his family was leaving him at home for a couple of days, both of them were quick to say that it wouldn't do for Michelle to visit his house.

The arrangement they worked out was that after his Thursday afternoon class, Hammett would walk from his office a few blocks over to a shopping center parking lot where Michelle would wait for him. Her aunt and uncle had just given her a second-hand car for her birthday because they'd promised her one if she wouldn't smoke or drink until she was twenty-one.

I was amazed that anybody could get to be twenty-one without smoking or drinking, but Michelle just shook her head at me and muttered, "I never thought about it. It wasn't hard." I raised my glass to her, she raised hers to me, and we toasted the young woman she had been.

Thursday worked out just as they had wanted it; they even got warm, sunny weather for their trip. When he reached the parking lot, Hammett looked all around to make certain no one he knew was there before he stepped into Michelle's car. To keep from being seen while she drove out of Boise, he lay down in the seat with his head in her lap. Michelle said that was the part of it that later hurt her the worst to remember, driving her car with the weight of Hammett's head on her right thigh.

She said that as she drove, they talked, mostly about their families and the way they had been brought up, Hammett an only child in Chevy Chase, Maryland, and Michelle the second of five children in Spirit Lake. His mother worked for the Department of the Interior, his father for the Department of Justice; her father, with two of her uncles, ran the biggest building supplies business in northern Idaho. So much did Michelle like the talking with Hammett that she asked him not to sit up even after they were well out of town. That way, she didn't think he'd notice when she started driving slower to make the trip last longer.

Little Sawtooth Falls was a tiny park tucked away in the side of a fair-sized mountain. The state had put up only a couple of small signs marking the turnoffs to it and had cleared out a ten-space parking area. When they stepped out of the car and stretched in the warm air, it was just as Michelle had thought it would be; they had the park to themselves. Hammett came around to her side, grinning at her. A small sign pointed toward the path to the falls. She touched his arm and turned him in that direction. They walked slowly out of the late afternoon sunlight into the deep Aspen shade and the smell of the mountain water.

The path wound along a stream that a rock formation prevented them from seeing, but the stream's noise grew louder as they moved through the trees. They descended a set of stone steps to a small wooden bridge. When they stood in the middle of the bridge and looked back up the way they'd come, the whole of Little Sawtooth Falls opened up to them, this immense, narrow chasm through which water billowed in tiers down to a pool spilling over right at eye level, then plunging to another deep green pool immediately below the bridge. Sunlight shafted through the trees; mist rose from the white water and the pools; high walls of gray rock jutted up to the sky.

For long minutes they stood there, Hammett just smiling and looking around them and she pretending to look down at the water, but mostly sneaking looks at him.

In noticing his glasses, she remembered how alive he was in class without them; so she reached up to take them off him. He seemed very boyish to her then. Hammett smiled at her and said she'd have to help him navigate.

Hammett's depending on her to help him move appealed to Michelle. She put his glasses in her skirt pocket, took his hand, and led him up the path on the other side of the bridge. Over there was a steep set of stone steps leading to a single bench where they could sit, where they could see the bridge and the stream far below them winding down through the trees and rocks away from the falls. The bench was a quirky fixture, something a ranger might have put up on his own because he'd decided that spot would be the ideal place to sit and study Little Sawtooth Falls. In front of Hammett and Michelle, maybe fifteen yards away, a powerful column of water caught the last sunlight of the day in a cloud of rising mist.

That bench was one reason why Michelle claimed a spiritual ownership of the place: every other time she'd come to Little Sawtooth Falls, it had been unoccupied. Sitting there with Hammett was utterly natural to her; in no place in the world would she have felt more at home. She joked with him that this was her office, and now she was holding office hours.

With their talking and stopping to kiss and touch each other, the time passed without their noticing it. Hammett didn't have to be back home, because his family was in Portland. And

Michelle's suitemates might have wondered where she was, but even if she did still live in a dorm, she was a senior and could do what she wanted. She figured her suitemates would be delighted if she stayed out late for the first time since they'd known her.

The light very slowly sifted up out of the woods around them, so that when they first noticed it, they were softly encased in a deep blue grayness, but they could look up through the leaves and limbs and still see a lighted sky. They were pleased with themselves for having forgotten about time. The darkness brought them still closer to each other.

She kept thinking that she was embarrassed by what they began to do, but instead of holding her back, the embarrassment fueled her desire to go further, to do more. It wasn't something either one of them would have even thought possible, but somehow they managed to have intercourse on that bench. This wasn't easy for her to tell me about—there was a lot of stopping on her part and a lot of questioning from me, but finally she made it clear to me how things went. It was Michelle's first real sex, and though aroused, she wasn't as satisfied by it as Hammett apparently was. But she was able to give herself over to the deep twilight, the sound of the water, the smell of the woods, the absolute aloneness and intimacy of the two of them.

When they stood up to leave, they realized they might as well have been blind. No light came from the sky, from the water, from the road, no light came from anywhere: it was the darkest kind of dark.

The situation was funny to them, a little trick they'd played on themselves—or rather a trick desire had played on them. When they started inching their way down the hill in the direction of the bridge, they were holding onto each other's hands and even giggling nervously. Their feet hadn't located the stone steps that had brought them up there—those steps had probably been set by hand into the mountainside by the ranger who'd installed the bench in the first place, but that ranger had probably never imagined two people getting themselves stuck up there in the dark.

Hammett was in front, stepping gingerly and teasing Michelle about having stolen his glasses. She was teasing him back, saying that if he had them, he'd just be worse off because it would only mean that he'd have a clearer vision of the dark.

Michelle realized she was shivering; she knew some of it was because of that mountain coolness that rises up out of the ground. She also realized how all of her senses had opened up, so that she was like this night-blooming plant that had become sensitive to even the slightest current of air.

She was a little scared, but mostly she was excited by the adventure, by the sheer craziness of what she and Hammett were doing. Until recently, she could not have dreamed of moving through absolute dark in the company of a man with whom she'd just made love.

The sound of the water was clearly audible; all they had to do was slowly make their way down the slope in that direction; eventually they'd find the little bridge. Then the path up the other side would be easy.

While Michelle was imagining their coming down to the bridge, imagining the way their footsteps would sound on the flat wooden planks, Hammett's hand slipped out of hers.

Hammett hadn't spoken, hadn't made a sound; he was just suddenly gone.

Down the hill from her there was a little noise, a scraping like a foot sliding through loose dirt and rocks. Then from farther down the slope there came a slight brushing sound like a shoulder scraping the bark of a tree. That was it.

Michelle stood still a moment, listening. She called Hammett's name, softly at first, then louder. He wouldn't play a joke on her; if he wasn't answering, she knew he must be hurt. Fear was rising in her so that if she didn't do something to stop it, she was going to start shaking.

Getting down on her hands and knees, she crawled slowly in the direction she thought Hammett had fallen.

Almost immediately she came to a drop-off of about a foot and a half from one shelf of rock to another. Michelle encountered it with a hand reaching out and down into nothing until she was touching the ground with her shoulder. If she'd been walking, she'd have pitched forward off that shelf the same as Hammett had. So finding it that way made her feel both worse and better. She figured Hammett had knocked himself unconscious somewhere farther down the slope. That brought the fear rising back up in her. But she also figured that worming her way down the slope the way she was doing was probably safe, and that going as she was, even if it took hours, finally she was sure to find him.

It did take hours—or it seemed like hours to Michelle. As she made her way downhill, the noise of the water kept getting louder. Finally she reached the top edge of a cliff-face that plummeted all the way to the water. By now she had been crawling through the dark, blind and alone and scared, for too long to be able to feel much of anything new. But when she stretched her arm down over the cliff-face, she said it was like that huge pit of rock opened up inside her. She backed away a couple of feet and lay down in the leaves and dirt, curled up tight.

Too cold to lie there any longer, she crawled back to the

edge of the cliff, crawled in the upstream direction for a long way, then back in the downstream direction. When she reached the little wooden bridge, that was when she knew she had been holding onto this shred of a fantasy of finding Hammett sitting there, waiting for her.

By now she didn't know how much time had passed. She was shivering hard, sitting on the bridge, hunched over and hugging her scraped knees until it began raining. Figuring she might be in danger of going into hypothermia, she made herself stand up and start picking her way along the path back up toward the parked car.

It was just so easy to get from that bridge to her parked car. She hated how easy it was.

She'd been carrying her car keys in her skirt; taking them out, she remembered what she had in the other pocket. It hurt her whole body to remember Hammett's glasses, which she thought she could feel now, pressing ever so slightly against her upper thigh. She didn't touch them.

She got into her car, started it, turned on the heater, then sat there thinking. The clock said it was close to three. It kept raining. By the time she had warmed up enough to stop shivering, she had decided that whatever she did, it would have to be the right thing for Hammett. She tried to think what that would be. He'd avoided telling her much about his wife and children even though their pictures were on his desk and even though she'd asked him about them quite a few times. She wondered what that evasion meant—probably that he'd wanted to protect them from what he and Michelle were doing in his office. She took a deep breath and made herself think even harder about Hammett. It came to her then that he'd probably been afraid she'd want him to leave his family for her. She had a quick flash of hating him.

She wasn't sleepy, and she hoped she was thinking with a clear head. She had faced up to the likelihood that Hammett was dead, or at the very least, hurt badly. When daylight came, she'd go down there and find him.

Even after the inky blue world outside her windshield started lightening, she made herself wait longer, because she knew she'd need more than just a little bit of light. Still, the rain slowed daylight's coming; when she started down the path again, she couldn't see very far in front of her.

At the bridge there wasn't a lot she could do except stare down at the rock and water below it. The rain was soft and steady.

She made her way up the stone steps to the bench where only hours ago she and Hammett had sat. The rain had smoothed out the mud and leaves around the bench.

By guessing about what angle they would have started moving in, she found what she was pretty certain to be the rock ledge that had caused Hammett to pitch forward in the dark. She found some marks that looked like they were her knee prints from the crawling she'd done down the hill. When she came down to the side of the cliff, she couldn't see over it all the way to the bottom. Like the soul of a stone, a draft of cold air rose into her face.

Michelle wasn't about to give up. She walked downstream from the bridge until she discovered a path that led her to the water's edge. Moving beside the stream, she worked her way back toward the bridge, stepping on rocks and ledges, sometimes even wading in the foot-numbing water. "Step up here, stupid," she'd say, or, "Over there, over there!" She was aware of how tired her body was while her mind kept driving her.

She was able to maneuver herself under the bridge and all the way up to the edge of the pool where Hammett should have fallen. From that point, she was able to see all around several tiers of the falls and down into the water. Beneath the surface she saw no shape or shadow that could have been Hammett.

So she walked slowly back downstream, then up again to the bridge and from there to the parking lot and the car. She got in and started it. Now she put her hand in her skirt pocket to hold onto Hammett's glasses. There were no other cars in the parking lot; there wasn't another person around. Shivering, she sat for a while with one hand in her pocket and the other on the steering wheel. Finally she put the car into gear and headed back to school.

Around ten that morning she drove into her dormitory's parking lot. The building itself was almost empty; she saw no one who knew her by name. No one seemed to take note of her coming in, even though she was wet and her skirt was muddy. It was an hour in which almost everyone was in class; her suite was empty. When she unlocked her room—she had a single— and went in and closed the door, she stood listening to the silence, staring at the rainy light at her window. In a trance, she removed Hammett's glasses from her skirt pocket and set them in her desk drawer, at the front. Then she undressed and put on her robe. She had the shower to herself. She didn't come out until the water had stopped stinging her scraped knees and palms. Back in her room, she lay down on the bed to wait.

Her mind darted in and out of sleep. She stayed where she was until well after dark. Then she dressed in her regular studying clothes and went out. She was sure her suitemates would ask her questions that would lead her to something, questions that would make her tell them what had happened or lie to them or something.

In the bathroom, a girl said hi to her; two others, chatting in the common room, smiled at her and gave her little finger-waves; Michelle felt almost invisible. She began to understand that they hadn't known she'd been gone. If they'd thought about her at all, they must have figured she was in her room, studying or sleeping or whatever they thought she usually did.

Standing in the common room leafing blindly through a magazine, Michelle had the eerie sensation of having dreamed the night that burned so vividly in her mind. She swayed on her feet. Then she felt her body sharply insist that every bit of it had happened.

She wished that she'd had somebody she'd confided in about Hammett. There ought to have been somebody she had to answer to.

She knew she had to get out of that dormitory. When she put on her jacket, picked up her backpack of books and headed for the door, no one even asked her where she was going. She was already outside before she heard somebody call out to her, "Bye, Michelle."

In a snack-bar booth with her Shakespeare text open on the table in front of her so that she'd be less likely to be bothered, Michelle worked it through in her mind to the point where she saw that it wasn't likely that anybody would connect her with Hammett's disappearance. She sipped her coffee. If anybody was even going to mention her name with his, she would have to be the one.

She tried to read the signs of everything she'd been through since that moment in class she'd found Hammett looking into her eyes. She could feel herself wanting to tell it all to somebody, tell it just so that it wouldn't evaporate. But she couldn't help feeling that telling somebody would be indulging herself. She knew she had to discern the answer to one simple question: should she walk out to the pay phone in the hallway, make a call, and tell someone what had happened? Staring at the back of her hand, she stopped it from shaking. A vision came to her, of Hammett Wilson sitting in his office waiting for her to come visit him and smiling at the pictures of his wife and sons on his desk.

So she decided. And walking back to her dormitory that night Michelle wrapped that secret around herself like some kind of invisible coat. She understood that holding it to herself made her experience with Hammett something that was hers and only hers. She set her mind to what she knew wouldn't be easy, carrying herself in such a way that no one would suspect how her life had been changed.

Something she never did tell me about, though I asked her, was what it was like at school when Hammett didn't show up for his classes or what it was like at his house when his wife and boys showed up and he wasn't there. She shook her head, as if she didn't want to say. "But, Michelle, wasn't there a huge investigation?" I asked her

"Yes, there was," she said, nodding, but she went no further than that.

The last week of school that spring, Michelle made excuses not to go with me to the Moscow Hotel for our evening drinks. When I stopped by her place, she was polite enough in her refusals—saying she had vast amounts of work to accomplish in order to finish the semester. I was preoccupied with school-work, too, and so I didn't press her.

On my last morning in town, I called Michelle to try to persuade her to have breakfast with me over at the Moscow Hotel. She didn't need any persuading. She said she'd been planning to see me before I went back east.

The morning was bright, and we were both a little giddy at having finished up our schoolwork. Over our last cups of coffee, we were chatting very pleasantly, I thought, when Michelle startled me by taking Hammett's glasses out of her purse.

"You remember these," she said, holding them in front of her.

I nodded.

"These have been with me all this time." She curled her fingers around them. "I've kept them in my purse or else in my desk drawer, near the front, where you found them that time. I decided that if anyone ever asked me about them, I'd tell them the story, as best I could. That was how I worked it out: I wouldn't ever volunteer to tell anybody, but I wouldn't try to protect myself either." She spoke very softly, with her eyes almost closed. We were sitting in a dark corner but near a window that cast Michelle in a bright beam of sun, with flecks of dust floating all around her in the light. Her skin was clear and pale as a cup of fresh milk.

She leaned forward and asked in a near whisper, "But you know what?"

I shook my head.

She didn't seem to see me, but she went on anyway, still whispering. "I hated every single word I told you." She paused before she spoke again, this time so softly it was more like a message to herself than to me. "And I won't ever tell it again." She kept her eyes on the glasses in her hand on the table.

While we sat there, I had the oddest sensation of being with her and not with her. I had a sense of her making important decisions, and there was a crazy moment when I thought maybe she was getting ready to ask something of me; though I couldn't imagine what it might be, I felt a vague dread about it. I was pretty sure I would let her down because I wasn't ready that morning to be responsible for anyone but myself. But

Michelle kept her silence, and we sat still until the window's shaft of sunlight had moved well past her. When we stood up, she quickly tucked the glasses back into her purse, as if she'd just stolen them. She came around the table toward me, meaning to give me a hug, I guess, but I wasn't ready for that either, because I backed away, facing her with no suitable gesture to make except a stupid handshake.

Michelle and I hadn't pretended we'd write to each other or keep in touch. Watching her walk away from me, I couldn't help thinking about Hammett's glasses riding along with her in her purse; the thought came to me that she was going to drop them in the first trash can she came to. I shook off that notion, but at a distance, I followed her out onto the street and watched her dark figure steadily diminish as she walked away. With my hands in my pockets, I stood out there in the spring sunlight until I couldn't see her any more.

Lately Michelle's story has been coming back to me, not the way it came, through her twangy Idaho voice but with such a visual clarity that it might have been a movie I saw lots of times years ago. The telling of it those nights in the bar of the Moscow Hotel seemed to make her cold, and I guess it made me cold, too. I remember the two of us hunkering over the table, hugging ourselves and shivering.

But when Michelle enters my thinking now, I welcome her almost as if she's a source of warmth. I understand how her telling me her story released me into the world where, every day, people carry out their lives with their stories locked inside themselves.

At the time, I didn't realize how she was affecting me, and I'm ashamed to say that I don't have the slightest idea what happened to Michelle. I can't imagine where she would have gone or what she would have done with her life. In my first years of teaching, I hardly thought of her. But as I gradually settled into my writing life, she began paying me more and more visits; I feel as if I have finally begun to be able to receive whatever signals her story means to send me.

Nowadays, my mornings of solitude are powerfully informed by Michelle Gonyaw and Hammett Wilson. More than once the thought has occurred to me that they may be the shades who inhabit the wing chairs that sit opposite me, while I tap out my sentences on my computer. If Michelle is alive, I know that she must spend some part of every day of her life on her hands and knees, crawling over cold dirt and moss and reaching out into the dark. And I know that thanks to her, I spend some part of almost every day of my life lost only in my writing, while light makes its way into my living room.

The Page

RIGGINS, HIS WIFE, and two daughters checked into El Conquistador around 11:30 P.M., Tucson time. Riding up there from the airport in their rented car, Vicky, the oldest, noticed the jagged horizon, deep black against midnight blue, looming over the highway. She got spooked and announced that she didn't like "that mountain." She was fourteen and given to responding intuitively. Riggins humored her. They were at the end of their long journey out from Vermont; Marie and five-year-old Polly were asleep in the car; within twenty minutes he'd have a beer in his hand and when he had finished it, a bed and Marie's welcome company. "I bet it won't bother you," he told her, turning onto El Conquistador Way and steering the car up toward the resort's main entrance. "That mountain's not going to keep you awake tonight."

The Tucson Writers' Conference had hired Riggins because their main poetry man, Kirby, Riggins's old teacher at Columbia, had experienced fibrillations of the heart and had been advised by his doctor to stay at home. Kirby knew Riggins needed a little career-lift and so suggested his name. It was a classy conference, good money, a reasonable number of students, and the Conquistador would let his whole family stay in his *cassita* for free.

Traveling *en famille* was new for Riggins. For years he'd been on the road, picking up a few hundred dollars for reading at this college and that university, usually trying to string three or four readings together to make his trips amount to more than pocket change. Before this he'd always gone alone, but he was sick of the part of himself that after his readings drew him to the blond with the blouse open one extra button or the boozy redhead at the reception who'd be touching his hands and arms while they chatted.

At home, Riggins was so attentive to his family that Polly, his youngest daughter, sometimes called him "mommy" by mistake. That was the self he wanted to take charge of his behavior on the road, and so Riggins accepted the opportunity to take his wife and daughters with him to Tucson and turn the Tucson Writers' Conference into a family vacation. Marie worked long hours as an associate in the Dean of Students' office at Riggins's university, and she was grateful for the break. Long after they'd checked in, he and Marie sat in front of the *cassita*'s living-room fireplace with its blazing fake log, nursing their drinks and listening to the breathing of their sleeping daughters.

To get his writing done in solitude, Riggins had trained himself to wake early. Now he always woke around five, no matter where he was or whether or not he had in mind to work on his poetry. This morning he managed to shower, shave, and dress without waking Marie. She had trained herself to sleep through his dawn departures from their bed.

Dawn was just breaking when Riggins stepped outside his room and felt the air on his face like a splash of cold water. The sky was an aqua-tinted shade of blue that he knew he'd call tacky if he saw it on a postcard. Across from El Conquistador's main entrance was a grassy area landscaped with palm trees and man-sized Saguaro cactuses. The resort itself was constructed in beige-colored rectangular units that Riggins designated to himself as "shoebox architecture." Since he'd never been to the Southwest, it pleased him to find it so exotic and yet so obviously unsuited to his taste. This morning Vicky's disturbing mountain looked raw and shaley, as if it had only recently punched its way up through the earth's surface.

By himself, Riggins ate a full breakfast, signed the check, then went out to the main lobby to find a quiet corner to sit down and look through his packet of student manuscripts. He read until time for the first meeting on the schedule.

Riggins's picture had been in the brochure for the Tucson Writers' Conference. When he entered the Manzanita Room, he saw heads turn toward him and nod with recognition; he thought he heard his name whispered up into the machine-rarefied air. The schedule called for Riggins to give his public reading that night. Even though he knew it was because originally Kirby had been the one they wanted to kick off the reading series, Riggins was pleased to go first. Readings clarified his relationships with strangers. The ones who liked what he read would become openly warm, and the ones who didn't like what he read would stay away from him.

Workshops were from ten until noon, and even if he did say so himself, Riggins's was a triumph. In his early days of teaching he had taken bad poems as personal insults; his workshops had caused student authors furiously and tearfully to depart the classroom. Over the years, however, he had become wily; he'd found it was easy to ask questions that would provoke students to attack the work of one of their peers; then he could take on the noble role of a poem's defender: "Maybe you're right," Riggins would raise his voice to say, "that this line is weak"—and here he'd smile enigmatically—"but with a few changes of phrasing, look how interesting this poem could become. Now what would you suggest . . . ?" His basic pedagogic principle had become that with the right changes all poems could be made at least interesting—though in some cases the changes would have to be executed by a Yeats or a Keats. This morning the student-authors whose poems had been discussed left Riggins's workshop feeling that he alone had understood their potential brilliance. The student-critics left feeling that Riggins actually agreed with their points even if diplomacy had prevented him from openly saying so. Riggins himself, stepping quickly, departed the Joshua Tree Seminar Room, glided through the main lobby, and walked out into airy sunshine feeling slick as a good embezzler.

The afternoon passed much too slowly to suit him. He ate lunch and went swimming with Marie, Vicky, and Polly. They wanted him to go horseback-riding with them, but he convinced them that he needed time to himself to prepare for his reading. Actually what he thought he needed was a nap, and he had the room to himself. He lay down, making sure first to arrange his books, manuscripts, and reading-glasses on the other side of the bed. But his sleep was light and unsatisfactory. Eventually he sat up, put his specs on, and sighing, made a list of the poems he intended to read. He tinkered with the reading order for quite a while.

After dinner that evening, Riggins wondered how he would have managed if Marie and the girls hadn't been there to keep him company. Walking down the hall to the Mesquite Room, with Polly swinging his briefcase and skipping out ahead of them, Riggins hung his arms over the shoulders of Marie and Vicky. "You ladies have to hold me up." He slurred his words and leaned heavily on them until Vicky whispered, "Cut it out, Dad," and Marie, suppressing a smile, told him to stop embarrassing them.

After the conference director introduced him, to polite applause, Riggins took the podium. As was his habit, he poured himself a glass of water and took a sip before he started; this ritual gave him a moment to appraise his audience. The seats were filled, and people were standing up in the back. He thought maybe this was because many came expecting to hear Kirby. He didn't give a damn. If his stuff was any good, here was his chance to demonstrate it. If it wasn't any good, he knew he'd be paid anyway. He cleared his throat, thanked everyone for coming to hear him tonight, and began reading.

Riggins's poems seemed to him like former residences: most of the time he found them so familiar as to be of only slight interest. He wrote mostly about the place where he had grown up, his parents, and his brothers, though he still had some poems about Vietnam that he liked well enough to read aloud. Occasionally, in his readings, he'd rediscover one of his poems and relive the experience out of which he'd written; he'd find himself reciting the piece with intensity. Invariably after the reading, people would come up to him to tell him they especially liked that one. Tonight, in the fake elegance of the Tucson El Conquistador's Mesquite Room, Riggins found himself reading in that special way from the first poem on; as he gave voice to the lines, he understood what they really meant. He was astonished that these poems even held so much meaning, let alone that he hadn't seen it before. He wondered if maybe this revelation was the result of his having accidentally assembled the pieces into some kind of secret pattern that yielded illumination.

When he stopped, there was an instant of silence, followed by a burst of noise the like of which Riggins thought he had heard only in gymnasiums and football stadiums. He gathered up his books and manscripts. He nodded.

Strangers surrounded him. He caught a glimpse of Marie and Vicky—he supposed Polly was there with them but blocked from his sight by the people making their way out of the Mesquite Room. He waved. Vicky smiled and wriggled her fingers at him; Marie was caught up in conversation with the conference director's wife. Riggins tried to force his attention back to the people who had come up to speak to him, but the ones he really wanted to talk with right then were his wife and daughters. He was aware of merely mouthing "thank you" again and again, meanwhile casting his eyes over the crowd.

At the party in the Coyote Patio, just a step down from the main lobby, someone bought Riggins a beer before he'd even asked for it. He still hadn't gotten to talk to Marie or Vicky, but Polly found him and demanded money for a Shirley Temple, which exchange satisfied his immediate desire to be back in touch with his family. He finished the first beer quickly, and someone else bought another for him. His conversational remarks seemed to him more and more interesting. He began speaking at length. Half a dozen people gathered around him.

One of Riggins's pet bigotries was against Irish poets, who, he claimed, gave readings only so that they could hold forth at the parties afterwards and bully Americans into hearing their screwball opinions, dumb jokes and anecdotes, and barroom songs. Now he had to smile at himself; here he was doing everything he could to hold the attention of his after-reading audience. But at least he was in a crowd of men and women in none of whom, thank God, he had a sexual interest. He stopped talking and was just about to feel terrific about his pure state of mind when he realized that he was in fact aware of a petite, suntanned brunette in a black dress over to his left and that he had remarked the presence, at the far side of the lounge, of a tall girl from his workshop, much too young for him of course, but with fetching straight brown hair and bangs. Then he looked over the heads of the people nearest him toward Marie, intently talking now with the conference playwright. Marie seemed to sense his staring at her; she turned directly to him and gave him the smile he'd been hoping to see from her all evening.

Riggins clinked his beer bottle against the glass of the young man standing nearby. He turned the bottle up, drained it, and set it with the others he'd finished on a glass table beside a potted fern. The young man and the others around him gave him a quizzical look but seemed ready enough to share his enthusiasm. Riggins thought he could have suggested that they all try some Cossack dances, and at least a couple of them would have been willing.

"Mr. Riggins? Mr. Eugene Riggins?" called a smartly vested and black-tied waiter at the lounge entrance, holding up a phone receiver and standing on tiptoe in his attempt to locate the right man. Striding toward him, Riggins was aware of his new grey suit, his own white shirt, his correctly knotted club tie; tonight he looked the part of a man being paged in a fancy hotel. "I am the right man," Riggins whispered to himself. He smiled at the waiter, accepted the phone receiver, and jamming one hand into his pants pocket, he enunciated his name.

"Mr. Riggins. Eugene. This is Emily Zadrosny. I just attended your poetry reading. I wanted you to know that it was quite an experience for me."

The woman's voice was low and melodious; he figured her to be over thirty but well under fifty. His first impulse was to envision her as thin, dark, and beautiful, but he checked himself: an attractive voice is no indication of an attractive women.

"Thank you very much," he said, keeping his own voice as neutral as possible. He looked over the chattering party of writers' conference members and was slightly disappointed that no one, not even Marie, had an eye on him. He supposed Vicky and Polly had gone back to the *cassita*.

"You're very welcome." He heard the tease in her voice, chastizing him for offering only his manners in return for her compliment. "I'm a travel agent, Mr. Riggins. I've never been to a poetry reading before. My home is in Palm Springs. I'm staying in room 1570 tonight, and I plan to leave tomorrow morning."

"Yes?" Riggins said. He felt a slight heat fly across his forehead.

There was a pause. "Do you remember my name?"

"Emily," Riggins said softly. He was suprised that it felt illicit to pronounce those syllables into the phone receiver.

"Yes. Emily," she said, chuckling. "And what room am I in?"

"1570," Riggins whispered.

"Yes, that's right," she said. "Good night, Eugene."

He put down the receiver, glad that no one was near him. He didn't pause. He went straight back to the party. Mentally he shook himself and berated Emily Zodoski, or whatever her name was. Did she think he was some sex-starved midwestern prosodist? Clearly the woman had no concept of Riggins, mighty poem-maker of Vermont.

"What are you grinning about?" the suntanned brunette asked him. She must have sneaked up beside him, because Riggins was certain he hadn't sought her out. He'd actually meant to be making his way back to Marie to tell her about the phone call. He studied the woman's face: high cheekbones, dark eyes with glimmering points of light.

"I just got an obscene phone call," he told her. When she gave him a seriously querying look, he added, with a sociable laugh, "and I enjoyed it."

To himself he harangued, "Damn you, Riggins, are you still in eighth grade and can't pass up a chance to flirt?" In eighth grade he had been extravagantly bepimpled and ungainly, so that whenever a girl even glanced his way, he had made an absolute fool of himself. Nowadays, when he felt the need for humiliation, it was his practice to flail away at himself with those memories.

"I've had some experience with that," remarked the tall girl from his workshop. She had come up on the other side of him. Riggins found himself struggling not to gawk at her orange silk blouse, against which her nipples visibly pushed outward. "When I lived in Tuscaloosa, there was this guy who called me almost every night. He had this beautiful voice, and he was always so sweet when he started talking . . . "

A short man in a blue turtleneck brought a beer to Riggins and joined them, then another couple came up. And so there Riggins was, discussing obscene phone calls with the group and dazzling them all. The brunette and the girl with the bangs and the orange silk blouse kept standing closer and closer on either side of him. He imagined he felt their body-warmth even through the good wool of his suit. "So you see," he intoned in his best classroom manner, "it was verbal seduction that got to Eve. If the serpent hadn't been such a great conversationalist, we'd still be in paradise."

The girl with the orange silk blouse smiled and moved still closer to him. Riggins damned himself for moving his arm so as to brush against her breast. Had she not then moved herself so that even through her blouse and his suit and shirt sleeve, his tricep registered the light rasp of her erect nipple, Riggins might have stayed there with them, talking about dirty talk for the rest of the evening. But the girl went that slight step farther than Riggins could stand going for the moment; the phone conversation still working in his mind made this girl's boldness really trouble him. He excused himself, pleading jet lag and post-reading exhaustion.

On the other side of the room he found Marie and slipped his arm around her waist. When he gained her attention he persuaded her to leave with him. He knew she was disappointed, because in their regular routine she rarely had a chance to socialize. But he could see that she was reading the urgency in his voice when he told her he thought they ought to go back to the *cassita* to see about the girls. He suspected that she'd seen him talking with those women and that she probably knew the exact nature of his difficulty. At any rate she was very decent about leaving the party.

Vicky was up reading when they got back to their *cassita*. She was absorbed in A *Member of the Wedding*, had only about seventy-five pages to go, and didn't seem likely to turn in until she'd finished. If he and Marie had had any lovemaking plans (and Riggins was pretty certain they did), Vicky's being awake cancelled them out. It wasn't the disappointment it would have been to him ten years ago. Nowadays he appreciated their sweetly companionable bedtime rituals. What they talked about was usually something of small consequence, but there was such a naked ease in their voices that Riggins found it satisfying. Tonight she told him what this person and that person said about his reading, all of it high praise.

"And what did you think?" he asked her.

Marie actually blushed. She had just sat down on the bed, about to swing around under the covers, but now she stood up and glanced out through the curtains, as if she thought someone might have been out there trying to spy on them. "I thought I finally saw what you've been doing in your poetry."

"And?"

"It made me feel bad that I hadn't seen it before." She turned toward him. He could see that it was hard for her to say these things. "And that I hadn't tried to help you more."

Riggins reached for her and stroked her shoulders. "You think I could have gotten any of those damn things written if it hadn't been for you?" he asked her.

Marie put her head on his shoulder and murmured that she didn't know.

From the doorway Vicky cleared her throat. She was leaning against the doorjamb, holding her book up and pretending to read it. For a nightgown she was wearing Riggins's complimentary extra-large, grey Tucson Writers' Conference T-shirt. "No disgusting scenes, please," she said.

"Why are you standing there, violating our privacy?" Riggins used his mock stern voice. He didn't really mind her being there, but he thought all adolescents needed a daily issue of parental harassment.

"Have to go to the bathroom," Vicky told him, still not looking away from her book, but walking now into the bathroom. Riggins and Marie exchanged glances and shrugs. They didn't say it, but they had to admit there was only the one bathroom, and there was only the one way to get to it, through their bedroom.

But after Vicky had returned to her fold-out sofa in the living room, after Riggins and Marie had turned out their lights and he'd curled around her back, and long after Marie had begun breathing deeply, Riggins's mind was constructing visions of Emily whatever her name was. He cursed her. He tempted himself with prurient scenarios featuring first the suntanned brunette and then the tall girl with the bangs and the orange silk blouse. But his brain was relentless: 1570 came to him like the words of a lousy song he couldn't stop humming, 1570 in that low, melodious phone-voice. You walk up to the door of 1570, you knock, and she opens it. She is . . .

Most likely she was an odious specimen. After all who makes that kind of a play for a man? *Zadrosny*, that was her name wasn't it? A fat, springy-haired twit of a woman, draped in a see-through, fuchsia nightgown and with a face like a pit-bull. A skinny prune-head in a mauve jumpsuit. Riggins constructed a parade of unattractive women, amused himself to the point where he was about to start snorting out loud in the bed, but got no closer to sleep. Travel agent, my big toe, he thought, sitting up on his side of the bed. Palm Springs, my right cheek!

In the dark, Riggins walked gingerly out to the bar in the living room, located the information folder for the El Conquistador, and took it back in through his own bedroom and into the bathroom. What he thought he needed was a definite piece of information about her that would put her to rest in his mind. With the light on in there, he inspected the chart indicating the resort's layout and located room 1570; it was in the next block of suites, almost directly across from the Riggins family. He figured that from the door of his *cassita* he could see the back windows of Emily Zadrosny's *cassita*. He wanted badly to get to sleep. Leaving the bathroom light on and the bathroom door cracked just enough to spill a little bit of light into his room, he located and retrieved his suit-pants and his white shirt. He wanted his shoes, but to encourage his wife and daughters to pack lightly, he'd taken only the one pair of shoes, and now they were beside the bed on the side where Marie was sleeping. He went back into the bathroom and dressed. Then he turned the light out and pausing after each step to listen to Marie's breathing, he tiptoed out of the bedroom and through the *cassita* hallway to the main door. Turning the doorknob, he imagined he could hear Vicky on the fold-out sofa and Polly on the roll-away cot, deeply breathing in the living room.

Then he was out in the chilly air, the Arizona sky so star-speckled that it outshone the feeble outdoor lights of El Conquistador. Vicky's mountain once again was a disturbingly large, dark presence on the horizon. For a while Riggins just stood there, bare-footed, looking up through the lighted corridors of space. He guessed it was around two in the morning. Then trying to remember the resort map, he set himself the project of locating the back windows of Emily Zadrosny's *cassita*. Riggins's plan was simply to see it, to stand there and look at it until he possessed that one object of knowledge: *the woman who had me paged is there in that room.* Then he could forget her. But he hadn't brought the chart out with him, and now he wasn't sure which set of windows was the right one.

He'd gone this far. Even though he was barefooted, he knew he had to go farther if he wanted to sleep tonight. His feet registered every cold pebble as he stepped antelope-style around the silly hard-surfaced pathway to the other side of that block of buildings. The temperature was probably just above freezing, and he was in his shirtsleeves in addition to being without shoes. Uncomfortable as he was, he figured he probably wouldn't get frostbite. The first *cassita* in that block was 1575. He padded slowly down the hill until he came to 1570. He stood facing the door. Cold, cold air chattered at his skin and especially at his vulnerable feet. Above Emily Zadrosny's door there was a light, but Riggins stayed out of its shining. The night full of stars sailed above his head. The mountain was enormously present on the horizon. He was of no more significance than some desert rodent, quivering out there under the surveillance of a barn owl. His wife and daughters, asleep some forty yards away, would not recognize the creature who stood out here in the shadow, facing the doorway of a woman who'd spoken maybe twenty-five words to him over the telephone. His feet sent pain spiking up through his ankles like shots of poison.

If he knocked, Emily Zadrosny would wake but lie still waiting to see if the sound came again, and after he knocked that second time, she would rise from bed and come to the door and hook the chain latch and then crack open the door to see who was there. When she saw him, she would undo the chain latch to open the door for him. She would be sleepy, a plain-faced woman but not ugly. She'd have short brown hair, and the black nightgown she'd be wearing would bare her intricately shaped, pale shoulders. "You must be freezing," she would say, hugging herself there in the open doorway, and Riggins would say, "Yes, I am," and step forward into her room. It would be warm in there. My Christ, it would be warm in there.

He knew it was because of his poor, bare feet that he had to turn away from Emily Zadrosny's doorway. Out under a million stars, Riggins decided to go ahead and have himself a cry over how much his feet hurt. By the time he had hobbled around to the doorway to his own *cassita*, he had stopped. In his hip pocket he had a handkerchief, which he used to wipe his eyes and blow his nose. In his shirt pocket he had the plastic card that served as a room key.

He let himself into his *cassita*, absurdly grateful for its warmth. When he eased the door shut, there was no more light. But he sat down right there on the hallway floor and rubbed his feet through stages of more and then less and less pain. After a while, seeing nothing, and with his heartbeat and his body temperature back to normal, he suddenly got the crazy notion that with all that foot-rubbing, he might have dissolved himself into the dark. He stood up suddenly enough to jolt his heart, steadied himself, and felt along the foyer wall with his fingertips.

Rounding a corner into the living room's deep grey light, he felt a lot better. It was nothing for him to ghost-walk his way along the wall, past where Vicky and Polly slept, and into the bedroom. It was nothing at all for him quietly to shed his pants and shirt. Then he was in bed with Marie who stirred only slightly. He didn't dare curl around her, but the sheets and blankets immediately began conveying her warmth to him. And it was only a moment before Riggins was ravished by sleep.

Collision

RIGGINS AND MARIE whanged their two cars into e
other downtown. They each thought it was the other's fa
and for a little while they stood out there by her bashed-in d
and his crumpled fender, yelling in the public dayligh
South Winooski Street. A big man in his usual baggy swe
and chinos, Riggins shook his finger in Marie's face. Marie
her heels and her brand new green dress from Nan Patric
just stood there with her hands on her hips and shouted bac
him about what a lousy driver he'd been ever since she
him in college and how she wished she'd told him that tw
years ago.

They had been one of those couples who rarely went bey
polite disagreement. One evening last year Riggins had s
his dinnerplate frisbee-style from where he sat at the t
through the breakfast nook and shattered it against a kitc
cabinet, thereby frightening four-year-old Polly into clim

into her mommy's lap to cry. And nine years ago, when Vicky had been five, Marie had told Riggins to take his TV and his football games and go to hell, had left the house just after she'd started cooking Sunday dinner, and hadn't come home until well past ten-thirty. They saw these as normal domestic episodes. These were things they'd done that they could laugh about at their friends' dinner parties.

But now there was this wreck. The two young policemen, smirking like teenagers, put away their notebooks once they found out Riggins and Marie were man and wife. Marie had been on her way back up to the university, having enjoyed a very pleasant lunch with her counterpart, an associate dean of students at Plattsburgh State College across the lake. Riggins had been bored that afternoon after teaching his classes and so had gone downtown to browse the CD racks at Pure Pop. He hadn't found a thing he wanted to buy. He was coming out of the parking lot there by the Nickleodeon Theater, and he'd seen Marie coming all right, but she'd had her signal light on and had even started cutting over into the left lane . . . Both cars were drivable so that they didn't have to call wreckers. But God knew what their insurance company was going to do.

That evening Riggins was cooking their weekday dinner as usual when Marie came in from work. He was still so mad he was whispering mean comments to his boiling pot of macaroni, but it surprised him when Marie walked right past the kitchen to the living room and sat down to read the paper without apologizing or even saying hello to him. When he called everybody to the table, Marie purposely avoided looking him in the eye. Toward the girls, who were picking at each other, he made himself speak with elaborate good manners. He could tell that Marie was just pretending to listen first to Polly's case against Vicky—Vicky had told her to shut up—

and then to Vicky's defense and case against Polly—Polly had been whispering outside her door while she was taking a nap. Normally Riggins would have told both girls to hush and eat, and Marie would have interrupted any whining plea for an exception to be made for the green beans with a "Do what your father told you to."

Now Riggins sat there stonily observing his daughters figuring out that their parents were passing through some weird phase that meant they'd get dessert no matter what they left on their plates. Vicky and Polly stopped quarreling and picking at their food; the two of them exchanged collaborative nods across the table. In that moment Riggins saw clearly how they were just out for number one. They picked up their plates and carried them into the kitchen. Their sly faces made it evident to Riggins that they had learned to pursue their own desires without regard for anyone else. He heard them scraping the uneaten food he had cooked for them into the trash. He heard them quietly assaulting the new package of cookies they knew they weren't supposed to open until all the old ones were gone. The corruption of his daughters made him so sick he couldn't eat, and he couldn't remember when he'd ever been this upset. Marie just sat there squinting at the plants lined up in front of the dining room windows. Riggins thought he might stand up and begin bellowing.

Marie suddenly turned a face of pure fury on him and snapped, "I'd win if we went to court."

"What?" he blurted, though he'd heard her perfectly well. He was stunned by what she said and how she looked, but he went on, "Like hell you would! There were witnesses who saw your signal light blinking!"

It occurred to Riggins that this was the moment to laugh, but that moment passed immediately, and then he knew that it would have taken only a remark or two more to have the two of them going at each other with the steak knives that rested inches from their hands. Marie's eyes were locked on his face. He heard Vicky tip-toeing upstairs to her room and Polly going downstairs to watch TV. He was shocked at what was going on right there at his dining room table. He almost said, *My God, this is worse than divorce,* but he kept his silence and kept glaring back at Marie.

Maybe it wasn't worse than divorce, but it was similar. From their closet and his dresser, Riggins gathered his clothes for the next day and went to bed in the guest room. And didn't sleep much. Which was all right because he saw from the dim light shining into the hallway that in their bedroom Marie was awake and reading until well after three. The next morning in the kitchen, they encountered surly versions of their usual selves.

Standing at the far counter in her bathrobe, Marie said, "This is silly," but in such a litigious tone of voice that Riggins growled back at her, "You're damn right it is." In his underwear, he was squatting before the open refrigerator, while she was making a point of not pouring from the pot of coffee he had just fixed. She made her own, *the way I like it for once,* her words never enunciated but nevertheless bitterly resonant in the kitchen as long as the two of them were in there together.

Riggins had office hours from ten until twelve on Wednesday mornings. It was mid-October and too early in the semester for students to start coming by to see him; so he spent his time in the office toying with the idea of calling his lawyer. He was freakishly aware of the power available to him while he sat there looking out his office window: all he had to do was pick up the phone and tell somebody at the other end that he wanted to end his marriage. One minute that was exactly what he wanted, and the next he felt as if he were losing his mind even to imagine a divorce. The thing of it was, his lawyer might also have been Marie's lawyer, and Riggins knew he couldn't stand it if Paul Martin had to tell him that he'd already agreed to represent Marie. But wouldn't she call a woman lawyer? Riggins pondered. His office was on the third floor of the oldest building on campus; he had a view of the city, the lake, and the Adirondacks on the other side of the lake. This was something he ought to know about his wife: the gender of the attorney she'd call in a crisis. But was this a crisis? He didn't call anybody for the whole two hours he was there. A sophomore girl came by to drop one of his classes. Riggins signed the form with a malicious flourish; he was sick of the entire female race.

As was their custom on Wednesdays, Riggins and his English department colleagues Hudson and Williams played racquetball during the faculty noon hour at the university gym. Middle-aged, bookish men, they were far from being athletes of any distinction, but they played hard, sweated, occasionally made remarkable shots, and sometimes injured themselves or each other. Today Riggins won two of their three games. Afterwards he became expansive, kidding Hudson and Williams about their age, telling a joke or two, actually having to shout his lines as they undressed in separate sections of the locker room.

After their showers, when the three of them were toweling off together, along with several other paunchy, pink-skinned noon-hour athletes, Riggins asked them how many feminists it took to screw in a light-bulb. When Williams chuckled at the question, Riggins chastised him with the joke's punchline, "That's not funny!" The men guffawed, and several of them repeated the lines out loud. Dressing, Riggins made himself shut up so as not so spoil his success. He hadn't thought it was that great a joke, but it sure had gone over well. He felt terrific until he walked out of the locker room behind two of the men who had laughed and he thought he heard one of them quietly say to the other, "What an asshole." Riggins had no special reason to think the man was referring to him, but in his crumple-fendered car, he sat a while considering the issue of whether or not he was an asshole.

Child care was his karma for the afternoon. At three he picked up Polly from the day-care center at the Y and gave in to her demands for movies to be rented from Jukebox Video; Polly chose *Grease* and *Dirty Dancing*, both of which she'd already seen half a dozen times. Vicky came home from school about quarter to four. She told him she'd had a bad day but wouldn't give him any details; in the kitchen she grabbed a soda and a fistful of cookies, then went to her room to make telephone calls. Riggins stood in the living room, gazing out the back window. He was aware of how inordinately he loved his daughters. But one was downstairs in front of the TV, sandblasting her brain with the most tawdry of American mythologies, the other was upstairs on the phone, idling away her study time by discussing high school drug culture while stuffing herself with chemicals and empty calories.

He turned to the corner of the room where he kept his stereo equipment and gazed at his records and tapes. Nothing was there he hadn't heard a thousand times. He stared at his bookshelf where there were books he certainly intended to read but not now. Then he stood over his coffee table full of magazines and journals. They weren't what he wanted. He stood in a trance, floating out away from what was supposed to be his own life.

Riggins knew that in his past, on a few occasions, he'd approached such a condition. It was almost always when he was in some strange city and in a motel. When it had happened before his marriage, he had called his mom and dad and chatted. When it had happened since his marriage, he had called Marie. "Whoya gonna call?" Riggins chanted and heard himself emit a bleak little chuckle.

When the phone rang, Riggins started toward the kitchen. But its first ring was truncated. He waited for Vicky to shout down that the phone was for him. She didn't.

Down in the basement the TV droned with the soundtrack of *Dirty Dancing*. Upstairs Vicky was playing tapes on her "box." He'd have preferred silence. Distant though it was, this cacophony in vertical stereo was torturous.

In the old days Riggins would have departed the house. Over the years he'd developed skills at the quiet glide out the back, the slammed door (both the front and the back versions), the brisk walk to a downtown bar, and the get-in-the-car-and-burn-rubber-the-hell-out-the-driveway. You didn't have to be angry to find The Exit deeply satisfying. Often it was a cure for mild despair or quotidian anxiety. Today, though, Riggins knew he didn't really want to leave his kids in the house by themselves. "What the hell would that cure?" he whispered to himself.

When he turned back to the window, out of the corner of his eye, he noted the presence of a gargoyle perched on the upper right corner of the doorjamb. Startled, he jerked his head back that way, but of course, the spiny little gray mass with an ugly face had disappeared. Well, of course, it had never been there. He shook his head and went back to gazing out the window at his back yard. Imagining strange creatures just at the edge of his vision was a recent phenomenon, one that he had thought to be almost amusing. Now, though the slimy thing wasn't visible to him, Riggins imagined it inhabiting his brain, eating away at his ability to enjoy his children, his house, his possessions.

"Daddy, I have a stomach-ache," Polly called up from the

basement. Her voice was both urgent and triumphant. It was a familiar complaint, but it could have meant anything from impending projectile vomiting to the child's having figured out what was for dinner and setting him up so that he'd excuse her from eating it.

Riggins went to the basement door and asked Polly if she felt like throwing up. When she told him that she didn't, he suggested that she lie down and see if that didn't make her feel better. Polly said OK. He stood there a moment, staring down the basement stairwell, rubbing his temples and thinking that he didn't feel very well himself.

When he came back to the living room, Vicky was kneeling by the tape deck in the corner of the living room. "You have to hear this, Dad," she told him as she fast-forwarded her precious tape. Her hair was put up into a pony-tail that splayed out from the top of her head; she wore an ancient navy T-shirt of his, old and full of holes, a pair of grotesque (fuchsia and chartreuse) tie-died slacks, and her high-topped Converse tennis shoes which she had tinted mint-green with an acrylic marker.

Riggins imagined some crude instrument scraping the inside of his forehead. He was in no mood to hear any sort of music that he could think of, but he knew it was crucial to receive whatever message Vicky meant to send him. So he sat down and listened to a song called "Stairway to Cleveland" that sounded like a navigator shouting to a co-pilot over the damaged engines of a World War Two bomber. The song carried out an interrogation: "Whaddaya gonna do about rock & roll, whaddaya gonna do about Ronald Ray-gun, whaddaya gonna do about Cleveland?" The part Vicky especially wanted him to hear was comparatively quiet; the buzzing instrumentation suddenly halted, and the shouter rasped out, "Fuck you, we do what we want to!" A rousing cheer followed but was immediately drowned in the recommencing of two or three sets of drums and about forty-two electric guitars. "Whaddaya think, Dad?" Vicky screamed at him over the closing bars.

In the paradise of silence that followed the song's end, Riggins told her that it had very nearly knocked him dead.

Vicky was so pleased by his response that she left her tape playing for him while she went upstairs to resume her telephone conversation. On her way out, when Riggins asked her who she was going to call, she shouted at him that Jennifer was still on the phone, they had just been taking a break so that Vicky could play that song for him. She was gone before he could properly thank her.

The music had an oddly positive effect on Riggins. He decided to check himself out by quickly glancing to the right and then to the left; no spiny faces glared down at him from either side. Maybe "Stairway to Cleveland" had driven the gargoyles from his brain. He didn't really know what Vicky meant for him to take from that song. He supposed she wanted him to be shocked by the obscenity of it, but he wasn't. In certain moments of his life, "Fuck you, we do what we want to" had been exactly his sentiments. He'd done plenty of what he wanted to, though he figured that he had almost never done what he wanted to with total disregard for what anybody else thought about it. For one thing, there was the matter of determining what in fact one did want to do. At this very moment what did he want? While Vicky's tape kept grinding away at his eardrums, Riggins sat there gazing toward the window and trying to imagine what he wanted.

He found himself thinking about Marie. The living room clock told him it was 4:30 now, quitting time for the staff up at the university, but Marie always stayed on a couple of hours. The dean of students measured his associates by how dedicated they were to their work, and so they all demonstrated their dedication by staying at their desks until around 6:30. Marie hated the policy but she said she went along with the practice because there was always work to be done. Today, though, Riggins thought she would put her files away, stand up, smooth down her skirt, pick up her pocketbook and her briefcase, cheerfully tell her colleagues goodbye, and depart the office. Clicking her heels out in the hallway, she'd head to the parking lot. She'd shake her head when she remembered that her car's passenger-side door was bashed in, but that wouldn't stop her from coming home.

Traffic would be thick at this regular rush hour of the city, and so Marie would turn on the car radio while she stopped and started and stopped again. She'd choose the public radio station, which would be just finishing up its afternoon classical music program. Today as she negotiated the corner onto her own street, she'd hum along a little bit with Act III of *The Barber of Seville*, which, of course, Riggins wished she wouldn't do, because her singing wasn't the greatest. But he knew that Marie always raised her untrained voice to accompany any music that appealed to her, whether she knew it well or not. Her impulse to sing along had given Riggins his first reason to tease her. In Charlottesville one Sunday afternoon, they'd been listening to Aretha Franklin in his old Jefferson Park Avenue apartment; when Aretha had proclaimed "You make me feel / like a nat-ur-al woman," Marie had proclaimed right along with her, and Riggins had said, "I didn't know you were a Motown girl," and Marie had grinned at him and sung it again, "You make me feel . . ." By God, they had been something back then, the two of them in their twenties, their flesh strung tight to their bones. Marie had worn a mini-dress when they'd walked to the Corner for lunch, and she'd caused so many heads to turn that Riggins had kept his hand at the small of her back and his own head held high. He'd weighed forty pounds less then. Now that he could see the two of them walking along the east lawn of the university with the great trees' leaves such impossibly bright reds and yellows in that October sun, he understood that he and Marie had both been utterly free that day.

He was startled by a shadow passing by the back window. He blinked and put his hand to the side of his head. He'd been silly to think himself cured by "Stairway to Cleveland." He stood up from his chair, meaning to go into the kitchen or out onto the back porch, he wasn't sure what he had in mind. But when he strode through the door and turned the corner, he and Marie were suddenly chest-to-chest up against each other. "You scared the hell out of me!" he told her, clasping her shoulders. Marie dropped her briefcase onto the floor and grabbed him around the waist. "You're the one who's not looking where he's going!" She had to shout because Vicky's tape was firing another of Jefferson Airplane's kamikaze songs at them.

"Look out!" Riggins told her, pulling her closer to him. "Damnit, I'm looking out!" Marie grabbed fistfuls of the back of his sweater. They clung to each other like Japanese wrestlers. Then Vicky was there beside them, chanting, "Isn't this song great? Isn't it just the coolest thing?"

Riggins said, "It's not a song, it's an act of cultural violence"; at the same time Marie asked, "Isn't anybody going to notice that I came home early?"

Just then Polly stomped up the basement steps, out through the door right beside them, and announced, "I'm still sick!"

"Are you going to throw up?" Marie and Riggins asked her almost in unison.

"Yes!" Polly shouted, grinning up at them, and all four of them grappled and clutched at each other.

The Meeting of the Tisdale Fellows

ON BROADWAY AT 113th Street, I am saying goodbye to Rosa Kingsland, whose hair is in braids and whose face has taken on the tint of a light sunburn. Not touching in the hot air, she and I lean toward each other, looking, looking; in the next instant our bodies will sprout tongues of flame. Goodbye, goodbye.

Rosa Kingsland and I never so much as brush elbows.

At Columbia in 1970 and '71, she and I were Columbia University's Tisdale Graduate Fellows, the students officially designated to possess "exceptional promise in the field of literary scholarship."

For nineteen years now, I've been a university teacher, for twenty-two a husband, and for fourteen a father. My wife is an accountant whose word is to be trusted; she will vouch for my being a standard-model life-mate. But teachers age, students remain young, and the gap widens. A teacher can become disconcerted. I often have the spacey sensation of drifting away from the green planet I know to be my rightful homeplace. In another twenty years I will have to perform the mental equivalent of squinting to be able to imagine what youth is like—or to remember what youth *was* like when it belonged to me.

Rosa Kingsland might have been the last love of my youth, though I suspect that it's silly to imagine you loved somebody under whose shirt you never even tried to sneak a hand. But why else would I remember Rosa blushing so vividly as she blinked into the greasy afternoon light of Broadway? Why do I think only a Beethoven or a Mahler worthy of measuring the sadness in our voices as we turned away from each other?

Idiocy, really, that kind of reminiscing. I know that. I also know that my ears still hold echoes of Rosa's formal voice shaping elegant sentences for her twenty-minute presentation in our Romantic-to-Modern seminar room. Without apparent nervousness, she spoke from notes neatly calligraphed onto a stack of unlined, white two-by-three cards. Her fingers scraped and clicked in counterpoint as they peeled each card aside, then lightly snapped it upside down.

Explicating "The Second Coming," Rosa's voice was a spellbinding coloratura, both gentle and precise. The demure poise of her slender arms, the long-necked tilting of her head served to underscore the rigor of her syntax. I estimate her English 542 presentation to be among the most intelligent nine or ten thousand spoken syllables I have ever heard.

Admiration is the beginning of desire. I suddenly knew why young girls threw their underwear at John Lennon and Paul McCartney. How did I convey my feelings to Rosa Kingsland? Later that afternoon, with my face twitching, I caught her eye in the crowded front barroom of the West End while Simon & Garfunkel offered themselves in falsetto as a "Bridge Over

Troubled Water." Among those shouting, beer-quaffing bar-
barians, it came to me in a flash: she and I were alike in being
helplessly civilized. I wasn't shy, but really, what could I say to
her? *Rosa, I know we're both married, but you and I are spiritu-
ally bound to each other. Shouldn't we go someplace and take
our clothes off and lie down?*

More reasonably, what if I had whispered to her, *Rosa, can we
go somewhere and talk?* and she had whispered back, *All right?*

In the very moment of our faces moving close to each other,
Rosa might have realized that I was the one wearing the odious
cologne she'd been smelling and despising all afternoon.

From that chaste April moment on Broadway, everything I
thought I wanted has come to me: my books have been published and praised; I have an excellent teaching position, a
pleasant house, attractive daughters, friends, good health, and
so on. I think it not immodest of me to say that I have lived up
to the promise I showed as a graduate student.

Of course sometimes when I go to bed, I feel that my day has
exhausted me, defeated me. But early the next morning I'm up
writing my essays, composing my lectures, grading my students'
papers, and discussing with Marie how to get Polly to piano
practice at the same time Vicky has to be at dress rehearsal.

When Marie and I moved out of Manhattan in the summer
of 1971, I was prepared for Rosa to disappear from my life.
That has not, however, been the case. Attending a colloquium
in Cambridge a couple of years ago and browsing in the Har-
vard Coop, I spied the name Rosa Kingsland on the spine of a
thin book, a hardbound monograph, really, of less than a
hundred pages, entitled *Yeats and Pound: The Poetics of Aggression* and published in 1978 by Hellcat Press of Madison, Wis-
consin. Small-press books of criticism are so rare that I might
have bought it even if it hadn't been Rosa's.

Of course I brought it home with me and read it straight through, growing more and more puzzled as I neared the end of the essay. There was the brilliance I would have expected in any words written or spoken by Rosa. But there was also a baffling obfuscation, as if her sentences simply couldn't bear the intensity of her insight.

The final pages of *The Poetics of Aggression* affected me queerly. I understood her argument, of course, but I felt as if, almost against my will, I were gaining access to a terror deeply held by the author. Rosa moved from her discussion of the verse of Yeats and Pound to a meditation on the Nazi camps and the symbolism of genocide. The book's last phrases were as follows:

> . . . *systemic hatred of such magnitude it took on a relentless rhythmic force and (if human will is the ultimate poetic expression) became a virtual poem-monster that literally crushed human bones, grotesquely synthesized suffering and brutality, praise and damnation, excrement and sunlight, but yielded no greenness of freshly conceived language, no bearable moment of new consciousness, produced merely that primitive sense of sorrow that the civilized mind can perceive only as a sort of frozen darkness—"Beyond Sorrow" we would name it, as if it were a city. The questions then become how thoroughly did such truly hateful poetry infect the basic poetic impulse of Western civilization and to what extent does contemporary poetry deserve the extinction our century seems to promise it?*

On the back cover of the volume, Hellcat Press offered the following note about the author: "Rosa Kingsland received her Ph.D. from Columbia University where she held the highly coveted Tisdale Fellowship. She is an adjunct professor of

English at Hamilton College and lives with her attorney husband, Peter, in New York State."

Several weeks after reading *The Poetics of Aggression*, I wrote to Rosa, offering my congratulations and such thoughts as I had that I thought would be of interest to her. I included chitchat about my teaching and about the book I had just finished. I addressed the letter to her in care of the Department of English at Hamilton College.

Probably there weren't many people who could read Rosa's book with any understanding. I could sympathize with her because I had reached a point in my career when I realized that there were maybe a hundred people in the world who could appreciate my deepest intellectual concerns. I thought that a decorous correspondence might be a comfort to both Rosa and me.

For more than a year I had no answer. Enough time passed that my writing Rosa and her not answering had more or less slipped my mind.

To become the productive person I am, I have had to protect myself from some of the ordinary disturbances of family life. My daughters are fourteen and five years old; they would pester me to intellectual death if I hadn't established certain customs in my household. One of these is my Sunday afternoons of doing the laundry and watching sports on television in our basement. Because Marie and Vicky and Polly have learned that I don't wish to be disturbed, they usually find things to do outside the house. Sunday afternoons I enter a sort of domestic coma. I keep the laundry room brightly lit so as to be able to see spots and stains on our clothes that need special applications of detergent, but I keep the TV room (the other half of the basement) dark. Lying on the floor witnessing the extraordinary performances of professional athletes, I empty my brain completely. Downstairs, it is always cool and quiet—I keep the TV's sound turned down so that I can hear it only by listening carefully.

I have come to think of this circumstance as my personal form of soul maintenance: I lie in the dark, I gaze at the lighted screen, I see no one, I talk with no one. I've found that my mind unconsciously penetrates the issues of my writing projects when I am able to let my thoughts wander as they will, without disturbance or distraction. When the phone rang on a Sunday some months ago, it was very unusual for me to switch the TV onto "mute," pick up the receiver, and say hello.

A woman's voice sounded, "Hello? Frank?"

"Yes?"

"Praise the Lord. This is Rosa, Frank."

For a moment I felt the urge to cry. I also suddenly felt strange to be lying down on my basement floor. That Rosa's voice reached me there as the blue shadows of the athletes flickered over me was simultaneously exhilarating and saddening. "Hello, Rosa. How are you, Rosa?" I liked saying her name out loud.

"Praise the Lord, I'm fine, Frank!" She sounded exuberant. "God made me dream about you, Frank. I saw you from an incredible distance. There was darkness all around you, Frank. It was like a mine, like an abandoned coal mine, without any lights, but God let me see down the long corridor to where you were, He made a light to shine on you, Frank, and I could see your face. I know you're suffering, Frank. I want you to know I'm praying for you. I'm going to ask my friends to pray for you, too. Peter will pray, too, if I ask him to. We're going to help you, Frank."

These words of Rosa's seemed to fall into my mind from a great height. Though I heard them clearly enough, I couldn't absorb what she was saying—or maybe I just didn't want to hear Rosa speaking Christianese. On TV, Patrick Ewing executed a power-dunk, got fouled, and belligerently slapped hands with his teammates as he approached the foul line. "Rosa," I said. "Rosa, do you remember that afternoon in the West End and how we went outside together, out onto Broadway?"

"I remember all of those days in New York, Frank, I remember every single minute of those days—"

"Do you remember how we kept looking at each other, but neither one of us could say anything?"

"Frank, those days are so clear in my mind, you can't believe how clearly I see them. They're like a nightmare I can't ever forget. The Lord took away my eyesight, but He gave me the gift of perfect memory, and He told Peter to look after me. Frank, when Peter and I lived in New York and went to school, when I took those classes with you and the others at Columbia, I was suffering the way you are now. No matter how much I used my mind, it wouldn't let me alone, and I didn't even know my own pain. But the Lord has let me remember it all so that now I can understand it. Frank, the Lord wanted me to call you today and tell you that I'm going to pray for you."

Rosa's voice had a thrilled sing-song quality that made me anxious. I tried to remember if she'd ever said anything about prayer or religion when we were at Columbia. "The Lord took away your eyesight, Rosa?"

"Yes, I had a breakdown. I was sick and in the hospital for a long time. When I came home, I couldn't see. Peter started taking care of me. Then my friends started coming to see me and helping me to understand how the Lord had saved me and why He made me blind. My friends helped me to accept that I'm on this earth to help people. Peter reads to me and writes letters for me when he has time. Peter read me the letter you wrote me. He got your phone number for me. I'm going to pray for you, Frank. I have to go now."

Even after the dial tone came back on, I kept the phone to my ear for the length of a Lite beer commercial, a Nike commercial, and a Pontiac commercial. When the receiver started making that incessant rasping that's supposed to notify you that it's off the hook, I set it back into place.

With the TV still on mute, I continued lying on the floor in the dark and staring at the running and leaping New York Knicks and Philadelphia 76ers. The house was empty, but the small noises of the washer and the dryer were oddly comforting to me. I thought I was probably all right.

If I wasn't all right, I expected I would be soon, as soon as the shock of Rosa's telephone call had worn off. Evidently Rosa was a born-again Christian; evidently she was blind. I tried to get used to those facts, though they seemed to deny something important about my own life.

When the basketball game reached halftime, I switched off the TV. After a while, the washing machine loudly clicked itself off at the end of its cycle; then the soft spinning of the dryer ended. I knew the clothes would be wrinkled if I left them in the dryer, but I continued to lie on the floor in the dark silence.

What came into my mind was a picture of Rosa in bed praying aloud. Her almost transparent eyelids were shut; she smiled slightly as her voice lifted in her prayer's sing-song current.

I felt myself peculiarly affected by this image. More seriously than I really wanted to, I asked myself, was I suffering?

"Not likely," would have been the sneering answer I would have given any door-to-door evangelist who asked me. "No, I don't think so," I would have replied to Marie, had she inquired of me in an after-dinner *tête-a-tête* if I thought I were suffering. But now it was dark, it was quiet; I was alone and flat on my back on my basement floor. Like the house itself, the question loomed over me.

Mornings when I woke up, I knew a thing that I sometimes thought to be pain. It was the opposite of my boyhood experience of sleeping in long after others of my family were up and moving through the house. Nowadays it was what woke me before sun-up, what wouldn't let me go back to sleep and what pulled me up and out of bed, even though in that moment of arising I almost always remembered the early years of my marriage when I would have turned to Marie at such an hour and begun nuzzling her neck and shoulders.

To call this thing pain seemed to me mere bourgeois whining. I got up early because I had work to do. I had articles to write, papers to grade, books to review, correspondence that needed my attention.

That very morning I had read the newspaper account of an American hostage—an academic man like myself—who had been beaten and kicked almost to death by his terrorist captors. Whenever I imagine the insane logic of terrorism, I quake inwardly. Reading of that man's experience had made me shudder, made me ashamed of my hundreds of daily comforts.

I picked myself up from the floor and went to tend the dryer. I'd put off folding the laundry long enough. I had some reading to do before Marie and the girls came back and filled the house with their noise and commotion.

That evening after dinner, when I had sent Polly and Vicky upstairs to prepare themselves for school, I recounted to Marie my telephone conversation with Rosa.

All through these years, Marie's face has remained youthfully pretty; she has a high forehead, high cheekbones, and a smile that I look to for reassurance. Over time, I have found that some of my wittiest remarks have emerged from my efforts to make Marie smile. But this evening as she listened to my light mockery of Rosa's born-again chanting, Marie's face remained solemn. She expressed little interest in the ideas I wanted to explore with her—the fragility of higher intelligence, the vulnerability of even the most sophisticated mind to religious fanaticism.

"I remember that pretentious woman," Marie murmured, picking with her fork at the shards of her salad. "And her husband who couldn't stop talking about himself." She snorted. "But mostly I remember the way you and she looked at each other when they made that presentation of the fellowships."

Apparently I had a more positive recollection of that presentation ceremony. "Rosa and I admired each other, yes, that's true," I said. Marie's tightened lips acknowledged the pique she heard in my voice. "But I'd hate to think we made a show of it to the outside world."

"Outside world," Marie murmured as she pursued some tiny scrap in her salad bowl. She sighed and put down her fork. "No, you didn't make a show of it to the outside world. But, Frank, there's something here you don't— Something you haven't ever—"

I kept quiet, though I felt a surge of excitement at what Marie might tell me.

Sighing again, Marie stood up. She's almost as tall as I am, a woman of stature, a woman whose figure has actually improved over the years. When she looked down at me across our dining room table, she took on a pose of almost royal authority. "I don't know, Frank. Maybe it's just something with academic men. The way you are with women—or the way you are *about* women. You've read so much about women and so much written by women about themselves."

I remained sitting and quiet. Marie, having talked herself into a state of mild anger, walked briskly to and from the kitchen, clearing the table.

"Your point is that we don't know women as well as we think we do?" I asked her softly.

"Yes, that must be what I mean." She stopped and stood looking down at me, musing. "But it's not so much a matter of what you know or don't know. Here, let me tell you something that happened to me a few days ago. Maybe this will help you see what I mean.

"After lunch I'm by myself and walking through City Hall Park back to the office. When I pass by the fountain, there's this long-haired skinny boy in a T-shirt sitting on a bench, strumming a guitar. It's a pretty day; so I smile at him when he looks up at me. He smiles back and in this faint voice, almost a whisper, says, 'Hey, pretty lady, show me your tits.'

"I stop and turn; I gape. I can't believe this guy. People are out, but nobody's close enough to hear what he's just said. I stand there looking at him, and he stares right back at me with his little wispy mustache and his little crooked grin. Then he says, 'Just kidding.' He turns away, but he keeps on grinning and strumming. Do you know what I felt like doing?"

"Kicking the hell out of him?" I hoped that was what she felt like.

"Yes, that. I wanted to do that and worse than that. But I also wanted to show him my tits.

"Jesus, Marie."

"I think the only thing that stopped me was what I had on and how hard it would have been to get them out there."

We stared at each other. I imagined her standing before the grinning lout in her light grey suit and ivory blouse.

"I don't get it," I said.

"I'm not sure I do either," Marie said. "This kid was a jerk. But whatever it was that made him say that to me was what you guys up at school have lost somewhere along the way."

"Well, thank God for that. But I don't see what this has to do with my telephone conversation with Rosa Kingsland," I told her.

But I knew she meant to be informing me that she had some understanding of the way Rosa and I were connected to each other back in graduate school.

On her way back to the kitchen now, Marie laughed and called back in to me, "Maybe I was just looking for an excuse to tell you about the kid in the park."

"Thanks for sharing that with me." With some effort, I made myself chuckle. Then I went straight up to my study. I wasn't about to tell Marie that until this conversation I had believed that only common women thought themselves to have "tits."

Disturbance lingered through my daily routines, so that I became aware, for instance, of my body's reluctance to climb the stairs to my attic study, of my eyes' flinching away from the computer screen I faced each morning. I began to perceive my classes at the university as traumatic episodes in which each exchange with my students included little jolts of pain I delivered to them which they then attempted to reflect back to me. Social occasions took on a hollowness that gave every hors d'oeuvre a bitter taste and that tinged the dinner wine with a whiff of kerosene.

Although they were ordinarily well-disciplined and quiet in my presence, I suddenly began noticing the most irritating things about Polly and Vicky. I realized that they had become infected with selfishness. Hearing them quarrel with each other at mealtimes, I could hardly keep myself from sending them both to their rooms.

What was acutely painful was my altered sense of Marie, whose every gesture now seemed to me suggestive, whose laugh at dinner parties took on a lusty tone, and whose facial expressions now seemed to me to border on outright lewdness.

Actually the worst of it was that on the surface, my days were proceeding in a normal fashion, but my experience had become relentlessly unpleasant. Each waking hour offered some form of abrasion. The music with which I tried to soothe myself was too loud, too sentimental, composed or performed too egotistically. On Sundays when I watched the basketball playoffs, my favorite players twisted their knees or took injury-producing fouls from bullies on the opposing teams. Around the office, my colleagues were insipid, spiteful, and obtuse. The university provost revealed a budget shortfall that meant a salary freeze for the coming year.

I was aware of the basic whininess of my complaints, was even aware of myself as having become high-strung and over-wrought. Nevertheless, I hurt. Admitting that I was powerless to help myself out of my emotional state, I took up therapy; at the end of the third session, I realized that talking about my problems with my kind therapist made me feel suicidal. Before the fourth session, I called and canceled my appointment.

Again and again I found myself brushing the skin beneath my eyes as if there had been tears there to wipe away. When I turned in my grades for the spring semester, I saw that I was about to face a stretch of time when I wouldn't have students and their papers to distract me from my awful feelings. Ordinarily I savored those weeks when the university's semester was over and Vicky and Polly were still in school and not likely to interrupt my quiet concentration at home. But now I knew that the last thing I needed was to be in the house alone with nothing to occupy my time except my own scholarly projects.

A morning came when I stayed in bed gazing at the ceiling until Marie woke up and murmured in her old friendly way, "Hey, look who's here!" I was about to confess to her that I was there because I was too discouraged to face the day, but Polly interrupted us by coming in with a request for pancakes. Marie hauled the child into bed with us, began tickling her, and saying, "Pancakes? I'll give you pancakes. What about these pancakes?" the two of them giggling and threshing the bedcovers, altogether too much rowdiness for me. I went to the bathroom for my shower, but at that moment I made up my mind to talk with Marie later to see if she thought I should take a trip or perhaps see a doctor who would prescribe a medication for me.

After Marie and the girls left for work and school, I frittered away the morning reading magazines and wandering around the house. The phone rang a couple of times, but I didn't feel up to answering it. At lunch I didn't even have the energy to take my sandwich and milk to the dining room. When the kitchen phone rang, I answered it only because it was directly in front of me.

"Frank, this is Rosa. I've been praying for you. How are you?"

It occurred to me that maybe Rosa's prayers were responsible for my malaise—like some kind of born-again voodoo she was unintentionally practicing. But then I was pierced with a memory of her face as it had been when she had caught my eye once during her presentation on "The Second Coming"—her animated, intelligent, utterly alive eyes.

"Oh, God, Rosa, I don't think I've ever felt so terrible."

"I knew it, Frank. For months now, I've been feeling your pain. Frank, I'm going to put Peter on the phone to talk to you. We're going to help you. Peter will tell you what to do."

Ordinarily I would have refused to speak to Peter. When I had met him in New York—at the reception when Rosa and I had been presented with the Tisdale Fellowships—I had found him a garrulous, over-confident, typically over-privileged Columbia law student. I specifically remembered his proudly telling me he was wearing his first Brooks Brothers tie. But sitting there with the phone to my ear, I was too numb to protest.

"Frank?" This was a male voice.

"Yes?"

"Frank, Peter Kingsland here. Rosa has persuaded me that she needs to talk with you. We've driven over here to Burlington. We're staying at the Radisson. Could you come down and talk with us?"

I tried to think what I should say. Just then the back door opened and Marie came in to have her lunch at home, as she does a couple of days a week. She gave me a little finger-wave and lifted her eyebrows, and so I whispered to her, "Rosa Kingsland and her husband are in town."

Peter's voice from the receiver called my attention back to his question. "Oh, is your wife there? I remember her. Perhaps she'd like to come with you. I'd enjoy talking with her while you and Rosa conduct your business, as it were." He laughed in a way that grated at my nerves.

With my hand over the receiver's mouthpiece, I spoke to Marie. "Rosa wants to . . . talk with me. They're down at the Radisson. Can you go with me?"

Marie frowned; I couldn't blame her. "I have to be back at the office by two-thirty," she muttered. I watched her yank open the refrigerator and reach inside.

"All right," I said into the receiver.

"So how soon can you get here?" Peter asked.

"Maybe twenty minutes?" I glanced at Marie, who nodded back as she opened her yogurt. "We're in room 544. Can you give us a call from the lobby?"

When I hung up, Marie and I stood where we were without saying anything. She ate her yogurt standing up and somewhat grimly stared at me between spoonfuls. My sandwich wasn't any good any more. I just sat and waited for her. "We'll go in my car," she said finally. "I don't want to be stuck at the Raddison if your talk goes on too long."

When we were almost there, Marie said, "I guess you're excited about this." She was in her laconic mode.

"Yes," I murmured. "I'm very excited." I wished I felt better about meeting Rosa, but I was filled with dread. Her born-again rhetoric was probably going to alienate me from her permanently and completely. I tried to call up some memory of Rosa that would make me feel better about going to see her, but my mind was filled with the image of Peter laughing, Peter now in his middle-aged lawyer's suit and two hundred and twenty-third Brooks Brothers tie.

He was waiting for us in the lobby, striding forward with handshakes for both of us. Indeed he did have on a gray suit with a brightly striped red and blue tie. He and Marie looked the parts of business associates about to attend a corporate meeting. I saw his eyes take in my baggy cotton sweater and uncreased cotton trousers. I could have sworn he winked at Marie. I felt a little jolt of hatred for the man.

"Rosa's in the room, resting," he said. "I thought I ought to tell you a couple of things before you go up to see her." Peter guided us to a cluster of furniture in the lobby. Marie and I sat beside each other on a sofa; he sat in a matching chair, catty-corner to us.

"As you know, she's been sick." Peter leaned back and steepled his fingers together just below his chin. "For a number of months she was in a catatonic state, almost completely immobilized. The doctors were able to bring her back gradually. It's as if her eyesight just hasn't yet arrived. So far as they're able to tell, there's nothing physically wrong with her eyes."

"What was the cause of—?"

Peter raised his hands. "Damned if I know. One morning I went to work with Rosa sitting at her typewriter, typing ninety miles an hour; that evening when I came home from work, she was frozen in her chair, staring out the window. She'd stopped typing halfway through a sentence. Since she wasn't talking, we couldn't find out what caused the breakdown. Months later, when she did start saying a few words, the Charismatics had gotten to her—"

Marie interrupted. "The Charismatics?"

"They're born-again Christians from all different churches—very intense. In Poolville, where we live, they visit every hospital patient who doesn't expressly forbid them from visitation. They visit every day. Since Rosa was this literally frozen human being for so long and since her family lived back East and since I had to spend a fair amount of time at the office, I went ahead and gave permission for the Charismatics to come to her room. Whenever I came in, one of them was at her bedside. When Rosa started getting better, she insisted on their being able to continue coming to see her. So now she explains everything as God's will. God wanted us to come to Burlington, Vermont, and pay you a visit, Frank. So here we are." Peter gave that laugh that I supposed he meant in a friendly way. The trouble was that it was plain to me that he resented this errand and that he resented me.

"You're humoring her," I said in as polite a voice as I could muster.

Peter looked carefully at me. I knew he was trying to read my response to the situation. "Humoring her, yes, I'm doing that." He nodded and took up his steepled-fingers pose again. "But I'm also hoping for some kind of breakthrough. Frank, maybe you don't know this, but you've been on her mind for years. She speaks of you with this reverence. She said that the class presentation you gave on 'Hugh Selwyn Mauberley' was the most illuminating experience of her entire graduate education. You're an important figure in her life, and I'm hoping that meeting you will shake her up." He paused another moment while staring at me. "To be specific"—there was a catch in his voice now—"I'm hoping that you'll give her back not only her eyesight but also her mind."

Then to my considerable surprise, Peter Kingsland's face reddened, his eyes squeezed shut, and his chest started sounding this awful "Huh-huh-huh." Marie stood up and went to him, patting his arm and shoulder. I didn't like her doing that, but there certainly wasn't anything I could say about it. It entered my mind that Peter was putting on a show for us.

"I'm sorry," Peter said, digging into his hip pocket for his handkerchief. "Forgive me, please," he said after he had regained his composure. Marie patted his shoulder once more, then stepped back to sit beside me on the sofa. She and I exchanged a quick glance.

After he wiped his face, blew his nose, and settled himself back into his chair again, Peter went on. "Of course it's not likely that this visit will bring about any change whatsoever. The doctors were careful to warn me not to expect too much from this, and you shouldn't expect any miracles of yourself, Frank. But even if nothing changes, at least Rosa won't be any worse off than she is now. Just talk to her. Do whatever she says. Humor her. She has this idea that you're in a bad way."

Peter raised his hand as if I were about to protest. "That's all right. Maybe you do need her help, Frank. Whatever. I just want you to know that I appreciate your coming down here and being willing to talk with her. Marie and I will wait for you right you here." From his jacket pocket, he produced a white plastic card and extended it to me. "Here's the room key. It's 544. Take your time. Please be patient with her."

When I took the card from him and stood up, I was aware of both Marie's and Peter's eyes on me. I didn't especially want to leave the two of them there together, but I didn't really want either of them with me. Just before the elevator doors closed, I saw Peter making expressive gestures while Marie smiled at him. Somewhat unpleasantly the sight of them reminded me of that afternoon on Broadway when Rosa and I had leaned toward each other so intensely that my mind had held us posed that way for twenty years.

At 544, I knocked and heard a woman's voice calling something that I took to be "Come in." The key worked easily. Then I was in the room's dark foyer, my eyes adjusting to make out ahead of me a TV set, a wall of closed drapes, and the lower ends of two beds.

"Come in, Frank." Rosa's voice was calm enough to make me feel better about the situation. "I think it's probably dark in here. Please come in and open the drapes."

Even ordinarily, even with the lights on, it's an odd sensation to step into someone else's hotel room. Though I didn't try to see her as I made my way in, I was acutely aware of Rosa's lying in the bed farthest from the window. It took a moment for me to locate the cords that manipulated the drapes. When I opened them, I was momentarily stunned; the entire wall was glass, and from the hotel's fifth story, what I saw was Lake Champlain with mid-day sunlight glossing miles of blue water, mountains in the distance, gulls soaring against a few white clouds.

"Don't be afraid to look at me, Frank."

I couldn't immediately reply. Neatly covered from her chest down, Rosa lay on her back with her eyes closed and her shoulders and arms in something white. I was shocked to see, in all that sunlight, that her hair had been cut short; it had also been recently washed and neatly brushed. Her face was as I had remembered it—as if she had been under a spell that had kept her from aging. She turned her head slightly toward me and opened her eyes. Now I couldn't look away from her.

"Please come here, Frank." She spoke very softly. As I moved through the room, her eyes followed me. I was about to think that my coming to her had instantly restored her vision, but when I reached her bedside, she lifted her arm and waved it helplessly in the air. It took me a moment to realize what she wanted; then it was easy enough to grasp her small, warm hand. "You're here," she said. I had forgotten what color Rosa's eyes were—so dark a brown that farther away from her I might have thought them black.

"God brought you to me," Rosa said.

"Actually, Peter ought to get most of the credit, don't you think?" I leaned down and kissed her cheek. "How are you, Rosa?" I whispered to her. I didn't want her to know how unnerved I was by the sight of her.

"Help me up, Frank." Rosa laughed a little, pushing back the bedclothes and pulling on my hand to swing herself up and around to a sitting position. I saw now that over plain white pajamas she had on a summer robe of white eyelet cotton. "I'm really very strong now," she said, standing up but continuing to hold my hand. "Let's walk over to the window, and you can tell me what it's like out there. Peter says there's quite a view."

Slowly Rosa and I promenaded around the made-up bed on our way to the window. She leaned on me, but she was too small to be any sort of burden. The skin of her forehead was as smooth and clear as a child's.

"I see this lake almost every day, Rosa," I said. "I haven't seen you since Wednesday of the last week of April 1971."

"Yes?" she said, smiling. We had reached the wall of glass. Looking up into my face, continuing to hold onto my hand, Rosa turned toward me. There in the room's brightest light, her face was exactly the face I had held in mind. Every detail of her dark eyes seemed exact and alive. "I want to hear your voice, Frank," she said. "I need to hear you talk about something."

"All right," I told her. She continued staring upward. Her gaze was so unwavering that I decided she really was blind. For some reason that certainty relieved me, made me want to make her the gift of the view from her hotel window.

"It's mostly shades of blue out there, Rosa," I began. "The sky is ordinary blue. But when you try to think what shade the water is, or the mountains on the other side, you understand that blue needs a whole language to itself."

"Like the Eskimo words for snow?"

"Yes. Like that. From my office window I can see this lake. Sometimes when I look out this way, I see the mountains on the other side just the way everybody always sees them. All of a sudden I think I see these looming forms behind them, the largest and palest blue mountains you can imagine, shapes almost too faint against the sky for the human eye to see. It's like an enormous mountain range over there in New York that nobody's ever seen before—ghost mountains, two or three times bigger than any in the eastern United States. A couple of times when I've thought I was seeing them, I've sat bolt upright in my desk chair."

"Nothing you see is without a meaning, Frank." Rosa chuckled softly. "Even being blind has a meaning."

"That's what you believe, Rosa?"

"Yes."

Her *yes* was a peculiarly flat syllable. Her expression became a frozen half-smile, her eyes open and directed approximately toward my chin. In the light, her ears and nose and lips were so perfectly shaped that I found myself wanting to brush her cheek with my fingertips.

"When will you go back to your work, Rosa? Don't you have another book coming along? Peter said you were typing on the day you—"

"My old work was a nightmare. God gave me new work to do."

"Helping people?"

"Yes." This *yes* was also inflectionless. The odd thing about the sound of this *yes* was that it could have been deeply ironic or perfectly sincere. I almost suspected Rosa of playing out an elaborate drama. But she'd never seemed to me a guileful person. If she were play-acting, her performance would have had to be one in which her belief was absolute. The obvious next thought came to me: in what way was that kind of performing different from mine or anyone else's?

"Rosa," I said, surprised at the emotion in my voice. "I don't think you can help me."

"I know that's what you think."

"My life hurts me—I think," I told her. "Or maybe it doesn't hurt me at all, I don't know. Sometimes I think what

I'm actually feeling is anger, then sometimes I think, no, really, it's fear. Then when I wrench my mind to try to focus on it, the sensation just seems to dissolve. I don't know. But whatever's wrong with me, I can't just sign up for somebody else's set of beliefs. Religion isn't possible for me."

"I know that." Rosa smiled up at me and squeezed my hand. The disconcerting thought came back to me, that I was as clearly visible to her as she was to me.

We stood at the window staring at each other for quite some time. I couldn't help thinking of Rosa and me leaning toward each other for that endless moment on Broadway at 113th Street in April 1971.

"So how can you possibly help me?" I whispered to her.

For the first time since she had taken hold of my hand, Rosa let it go. She held herself straight and spoke as if offering a formal recitation. "Frank, here's what I've come to tell you. My work was making me curl up inside myself. I couldn't just write. I had to feel it, had to go so far down inside myself to find what I needed to make my words matter to me. I kept going inside myself like that, I started curling up tighter and tighter, and I almost got caught in there. You know how mothers always warn their kids to stop looking cross-eyed, or their eyes might get stuck? Like that." Rosa chuckled nervously. "Except it wasn't funny, and I didn't know it was happening," she said.

"Let me tell you what I remember, Frank. I was struggling to write this paragraph for a whole afternoon, this impossible paragraph that I was just about to bring up out of myself, when all of a sudden I became aware of what I was seeing out the window. There was the butternut tree in our yard, then the neighbor's brick house and their little girl riding her tricycle on their porch. I didn't even know that child's name, but I was really watching her move out of the shadow and into the light, then back again, over and over. I felt like I was studying one of those tiny paintings by Corot—so vivid and so far away. I stared until my eyes started burning as if someone had thrown acid in them."

Rosa's face went blank then. She was the stilled oracle. What I felt was utterly strange to me. I became aware of some dreadful, decayed part of myself loosening. I remembered my parachute training in the army, that moment, falling through the air, when I could actually feel my parachute slipping out of the pack I had strapped behind me. The parachute's slipping away behind me had always felt exhilarating because it meant that the parachute was going to work, that I was not going to plummet to my death. I felt a similar exhilaration standing and gazing at this perfectly preserved Rosa who had come to speak to me. Something departed from me that I knew I had to leave behind.

Almost immediately I wanted to say goodbye to Rosa, as if I had been locked in this room with her for far too long. When I lifted my wrist to glance at my watch, Rosa's face became alive again. She seemed embarrassed, as if I'd just walked in and caught her in her pajamas. She crossed her arms around herself. "Brrrr!" she said. "Don't you think it's cold in here? Can you help me back?"

Of course I gave her my hand and led her there, holding up the covers while she slowly swung her legs around.

I sat down beside her, her eyes meeting and holding mine. I wondered all over again about her blindness. In almost a whisper I said, "You can see me, can't you, Rosa?"

A small smile came to her face but quickly disappeared. She stayed quiet for so long that I thought she wasn't going to answer me at all. When she did speak, the words were barely loud enough for me to hear. "Sometimes God lets me think I can see," she said.

Her face remained solemn while I thought about her. Her mood had darkened. Now I was ashamed of how good I felt, how eager I was to leave her. As if she knew my thoughts, Rosa turned on her side, causing me to stand up so that she could pull the covers up around her shoulders. "I'm tired now, Frank," she said, drawing her knees up, letting her eyelids droop. "I'll have to ask you to let me rest."

I thought about thanking her, I really did, but it seemed as improper as it would have been for me to leave money on her bedside table. I kissed her forehead and told her that Marie was waiting downstairs and had to be back at her office by two-thirty. I had to go.

"Do you mind closing the drapes?" Rosa asked, raising her hand to shade her already-closed eyelids. Her mouth turned down now, like an old woman's. "Are you all right?" I asked her as I walked toward the window.

She said nothing until I had pulled the drapes closed and darkened the room so that I could no longer make out her features. "Please tell Peter—" Her voice was weak. "Please tell Peter I need him."

"Goodbye then," I told her, stopping at her bed as I walked by to pat her foot. I could make out nothing definite, a paleness that was probably her face, shadows that might have been her hair.

I wasn't certain what she said next, but I knew she hadn't the energy to repeat it, and I could figure it out later.

"All right, Rosa," I said. "Yes."

I was quick to leave the room and ease the door shut behind me. In a few strides I reached the elevator, which was already there and waiting for me. Inside the metal chamber, swiftly falling, I experienced this moment of panicky disorientation, as if I were hurtling aimlessly through space. But my blurred reflection in the door reminded me that when it opened, Peter and Marie would be waiting for me downstairs in the lobby. They would be watching for me. "She'll be fine," I said aloud, practicing. "Rosa's going to be OK." I would give them a normal face and ordinary words, even as I stepped into the next dimension of my life.

Mister Mister

I

I AM NOT DEVOTED to my plants. I'm only mildly interested in them, and they are only mildly healthy. The aloe grows so relentlessly that sometimes I have to remove gross sections of it to keep its pot from tipping over. But aloe is just that way. Some of my other plants, my little cactuses, for instance, are disgracefully feeble.

II

Yesterday around dusk, I learned how to put the rabbit to sleep. He likes to have the front of his head scratched, between his eyes and up his forehead to the roots of his ears, then almost down to his nose. I was careful not to scratch too close to his nose because that disturbs him. So I sat very still, with him on the back porch window-shelf right beside my shoulder, and I scratched him until I saw his eyes were staying closed and his body was relaxed. When I stopped and kept quiet, he remained in the trance for maybe a couple of minutes before his eyes opened up again. I'm hoping I'll be able to hypnotize him like that again with my wife or one of my daughters as a witness. Then I'll be the unrivaled Bunny Master of our household.

III

Lately I've been feeling this desire to fall down. It comes to me in the presence of soft carpets and usually when I'm alone. But sometimes I'll be standing with my colleagues or some students on the grimy linoleum hallways at school, and I'll just want to collapse right there, not a hard crash or anything violent, just an easy folding down to the floor.

Beyond the fall, I don't have any definite ideas. I think I'll sort of curl up, but not into a tight fetal position. I'll probably be willing to talk, which of course will suggest that I ought to address the question of what I think I'm doing. "Oh, I just felt like falling down," I'll say, or something sociable and appropriate like that. I'll promise to get up in a minute or so.

IV

Perhaps I am giving the wrong impression by referring to them as *my* plants. They're not really mine—in a formal sense most of them belong to my wife. But since I've looked after them for so many years, I suppose I've come to think of them as *my* plants—as opposed to *the* plants, or *my wife's* plants.

The only reason I tend them is that I like to keep busy while the morning coffee drains through its filter. Since I make a lot of coffee, I have to find a fair number of chores to use up all that draining time.

So after I empty the dish-drainer and straighten up the kitchen counter, I walk through the downstairs rooms with the mister. I use this occasion to finger the soil of likely candidates for water to see if they really do need it. A more fastidious man than myself might be reluctant to insert his finger into the soil of a house plant. But I am all business and concerned, as I make my second round with the plastic watering can, with dispensing what is necessary for each plant's continuing survival.

V

The rabbit wasn't my idea, of course. Every year at the bunny tent of the Champlain Valley Fair, Molly, my youngest daughter, has begged for one. Every year, just about the time Molly gives up on me, I've been on the verge of saying all right. This year, I didn't give her a chance to give up. We were at the fair on the last day, the bunny tent had only a few people in it, and the owners were packing up the stock they hadn't sold. Most of those rabbits were pretty inert, even if you tried to pick them up, but when the lady-owner opened this fellow's cage, he stood right up and poked his nose out, clearly ready to go somewhere. We took him to mean that he wanted to go with us. When the lady murmured that she'd sell him for ten dollars, so quickly did I pluck the bills from my wallet that I startled us all.

He's a Dutch rabbit, with his body mostly black and his face, chest, and paws mostly white, about three-quarters as big as a standard white bunny. Though his fur has a slight barn-yard smell, the black of his coat shines, and the white of it is immaculate all the way down to his paws. When he sits in the sunlight, you can see the veins through the skin of his ears.

VI

Maybe nobody will mind if I stay down there on the floor. I can be everybody's metaphor. The environmentally concerned will see me as one statement, right-to-lifers as another, and post-deconstructionist phenomenologists as yet another. According to the needs and inclinations of my viewers, I'll be comic or tragic, minimalist, abstract, or overtly commercial.

VII

Occasionally I wonder what someone outside would think of my performance. For a good part of the year, it's dark at that time of day—around five-thirty or quarter of six in the morning. So say for some crazy reason you're outdoors and walking by this house with its lights on, it's cold out, snow on the sidewalk, slippery enough to slow you down, and you glance up through a window and see this guy about the size of a Division II college tight end shooting at the window sill, pulling the trigger like mad even though his weapon makes no noise. Maybe you stand still long enough to discern that actually he's misting his azalea; more likely, you skedaddle so as to be able to worry about it when you can recollect the scene in tranquility.

VIII

His official name is Ringo—by decree of Molly, his official owner—but he has picked up other tags from the rest of us: Matisse (my seventeen-year-old daughter's first choice), Pretty

Boy (my wife's), Bonzo Bunny, Buns, Bones, Dr. Bones (my preference), Rabeetz, Rabitzio, and Turdmacher. (This latter choice is usually exercised by someone cleaning up after him.)

Initially we kept Molly's rabbit in the box the lady gave us when she sold him. Then my wife bought a cage. Then we started letting him have the run of the back porch. That's his current circumstance, though he occasionally sneaks through the back door into the house, and we have to chase him down. Nowadays on his forays indoors, he heads upstairs for the guest room. We all like this choice better than his old one, back in behind the stereo rack where his inclination to chew wires recently resulted in a thirty-two dollar repair bill for the tape deck.

IX

Visiting the Metropolitan Museum of Art a few months ago, I found myself drawn to this life-sized black stone figure stretched out on the floor on its side. It rested among many other sculpted figures, every one of them sitting or standing. Some of this statue's power over me came from its place in the gallery's context, from its being a horizontal among the many verticals.

I recall that the lying-down figure provoked in me a mild anxiety because of its stiffness or immobility or statuesqueness or what have you. You really notice it when a supposedly resting person's muscles seem clenched. An upright figure can be frozen, but you can't help feeling that a prone one should soften into its pose, should yield to gravity.

X

Over the course of months the paper boy must have had to interpret this image—of the big guy at the window silently triggering the pistol with a huge handle and a tiny barrel. Lots of mornings while I'm misting, I hear him stomping up the porch steps. He and I have never spoken.

XI

Anger at a bunny has to be right up there with the most irrational of human emotions. I confess I've felt plenty of it. The chewed tape-deck cord caused a mere simmer compared to the rage he provoked with some rebellious toilet tactics one Saturday afternoon with company due in an hour and me trying to clean up the back porch. Standing over the third incorrectly placed pee-splash in ten minutes with your thumb and forefinger around a bad little bunny's neck, you tune into a surprisingly vivid memory of that Discovery Channel program where the hawk slashes down a rabbit and rips into its belly, then over a bloodied beak stares coldly at the camera.

XII

When I fall down, I'm certain I'll relax. That will be the point, really—to stop pitching myself against time and gravity, to give over to the surface of the earth. Except that I prefer lying on a floor to lying on the actual earth, which even as a child I found inhospitable (which is to say damp, buggy, lumpy, and itchy).

XIII

I've never even read a house plant book, and there are plenty of them around—a couple, even, here in the house, that my wife bought years ago, before we had kids and she used to take care of the plants.

I'm not saying I dislike these plants. I'm just explaining how their place in my life is one of small consequence.

XIV

He makes spongy-sounding little grunts and squeaks when he eats or when his back or neck is being scratched. But because he is mostly mute, Dr. Bones's primary mode of communication, I have concluded, is body movement. When he's feeling friendly, he runs in circles around my feet. Playful, he dashes back and forth in front of me and thumps the floor with one of his hind paws to drum up my interest in him. Bored, he stays put, or else gets up slowly, stretches, and turns his back on me. Afraid, he scuttles under the porch furniture. Curious, he extends himself toward me or even stands up to get a closer view of something I might be carrying, something he might like to eat. His body movements fall into two separate modes; for most back-porch situations, he moves at standard speed— fast, but not too fast; however, when he's in the house and really doesn't want me to catch him, he goes into turbo.

The comedy of a two-hundred-pound man chasing a pound-and-a-half rabbit through a house is probably lost on the rabbit, whose one- or two-ounce brain can't have very many circuits available for appreciating Spontaneous Theater of the Absurd. Still, the night he got into Molly's room and required my wife and me to crawl around the floor, flailing under the beds to try to capture him without waking our sleeping daughter, I wondered about the content of Dr. Bones's brain waves.

X V

I don't think this desire of mine represents significant personal change. It's a phase. When the weather improves, I'll get new urges; I'll want to sprint across the campus green or take off my shoes, roll up my pants, and go wading in the fountain. I'll want to sing my country and western songs outside the dean's office.

X V I

I admit that it is true that I take it as an achievement whenever the hibiscus graces the house with a blossom. It is true that I take personal credit for having saved the life of Edna, the ailing ficus tree. When she was about half gone, shedding leaves like a third-rate stripper, I performed major surgery on Edna with my garden saw, then carried her up to my study where she could recuperate under my skylight.

Finally, it is true that I'm the only one in the family who truly understands the fern forest bowl. I'm the one who picked out a yellow- and green-leaved replacement for the red coleus that couldn't live in it; I'm the one who can look at the forest and instantly know if a little monsoon action is appropriate.

X V I I

People who rattle on and on about their pets are not my favorite company, and so to non-family members I try to keep my observations about Dr. Bones to a minimum. If I like somebody, I'll take him or her out to the back porch to make an introduction. But even with my wife and daughters, I don't let on that I'm as interested in Bones as I am. In the privacy of my own brain, I entertain lots of fruitcake theories, a current favorite of which is that since it is clearly the case that we humans have failed to understand the planet and its creatures, then perhaps my relationship with Bones potentially holds the key to the survival of the human species.

The way I figure it, though, I'm not likely to discover the key, even if Bones goes into super-turbo communication mode and makes the incredible body movements that could reveal it to me. As a boy I was a serious student of Tarzan. My ultimate fantasy—cherished even more than the one where I mounted a silver-saddled palomino, waved goodbye to my parents, and began riding west—was to have a black panther for a companion. But the fancies of those days are invalidated by my adult life. I drive a Chevy station wagon, eat fast food, love appliances, can't be bothered to sort my trash for recycling, and waste a hell of a lot of water with my hygiene. A guy like me is not likely to be the recipient of the essential secret of the universe.

XVIII

Besides, I am the publicly declared enemy of the lemon tree that my oldest daughter planted when she was in fourth grade. The only thing that has kept me from throwing that spindly thing into the trash has been my daughter's pitiful pleading. I am also the one who truly enjoys slicing off the leaves of the amaryllis in the fall before I haul it downstairs to the basement closet to make it sit in the dark for three months.

XIX

But I can't help wondering—you know how silly ideas come to you—if in this slice of time I might be a kind of national symbol. Maybe my karma for the past month has been to be the quintessential American of the first quarter of fiscal 1990. Maybe the forces of history have randomly focused on me to induce this desire to fall down on the floor and lie there. Maybe I express what the nation wants right now—just to take a break.

In a day or two this symbolic duty will have to fall to somebody else. And this somebody will feel a desire of a different kind—to get up and do something that matters, to walk calmly into the darkness, to plunge boldly into the deep end, or to gaze up into the clouds and envision the beautiful city.

XX

At dusk yesterday afternoon, I experienced this holy moment, scratching Dr. Bones's forehead and suddenly seeing him like it so much he was snoozing off right there at my shoulder. I guess it wasn't anything remarkable. Cats and dogs sleep in people's laps all the time. The fate of human civilization did not crucially rest on my little back-porch petting of my daughter's bunny. I know that perfectly well.

So I should keep this to myself, too, but since I've gone this far in revealing my crackpot secrets, I'll tell this last one. There was a fraction of a moment there, with Dr. Bones's minute eyelids drooping and my finger brushing along the frontal bridge of his skull, when the lower threshold of my identity just dropped out of me and I became something only one or two evolutionary stages up from protoplasm. In the half light of my back porch, I was something alive and in accord with something else alive.

XXI

In conclusion, I want the record to show that I have never spoken so much as even one syllable to any plant in this house. Nor do I sing to them. There are those among them—the African violet tends to be especially vain—who might argue that my rendition of "Love Me Tender" has been performed for their benefit. This, however, is just the kind of egotistical misconception of which my plants are often guilty. The facts are that I am an Elvis fan from way back and that I enjoy singing to the empty house.

XXII

I don't know what comes next. I see only as far as my little downward tumble and someone kneeling beside me to ask if I am all right. Then I hear my happy whisper: "I feel fine."

The Hearing

SINCE DEAN POULIN has stipulated that this is to be an informal occasion and since I have been assured that, regardless of your committee's findings, my tenure is not under threat, I should very much appreciate the opportunity to tell my story in my own fashion. Thank you. I shall speak freely then.

I would estimate the time Honorée Evans and I spent together to be approximately two-and-a-half hours. Because, as you know, this was on the Wednesday before Thanksgiving, there were few students left on campus.

The day had been clear and sunny but also windy and cool. While Honorée and I were together, the light outside changed from a pale gold to a deep coppery tint. It was one of those stretches of time in which paradise returns to the earth. Or maybe one thinks like that only if one is an English professor approaching retirement.

As you must know, I was hired here as an instructor nearly

thirty-five years ago. My promotion to full professor came in 1982. I believe my reputation is that of a dedicated teacher who is respectful of his students. That is the role I have always tried to carry out. I've heard remarks that indicate that certain of my colleagues are thought to be lecherous, but I don't believe I've ever been numbered among them.

I call my students by their first names, and they call me Professor Riggins or Doctor Riggins. I don't encourage them to call me Mister Riggins because the *mister* seems to deny the dignity I've managed to achieve in my many years in this profession. Under no circumstances do I allow any undergraduate to call me Frank—as some of them did when I first began teaching in the seventies.

Honorée Evans is a student I knew about as well as any other in that section of Modern Short Fiction—maybe a little better than some, because she was attentive and her quizzes showed her to be an alert reader. Though she wasn't the strongest student in the class, she was among the stronger half-dozen of the thirty-some enrolled in it.

Until recently I didn't know a great deal about her. Because of certain refinements in her speech and her manner of dressing, I suspected that she wasn't a Vermonter but was from the northeast, Massachusetts most likely, and had attended a private high school. My class list told me that she was a sophomore. I knew she had a boyfriend in California whom she sometimes visited. One of the other students, a friend of Honorée's, once accounted for her absence with that information. So, later on, I teased Honorée with some references to California.

Mild teasing is a method of mine. I establish a rapport with most of my students. I don't try to get cozy with them, but I find that they are more willing to speak up in class if they realize that I recognize them as individuals. So when I return their quizzes, I initiate light exchanges with each of them. "No California dreaming today, Honorée," I might have said, handing back her quiz.

As a teacher of narrative, I'm sensitive to nuances of dialogue, suggestiveness, innuendo. I've become something of an expert at keeping that kind of thing out of my remarks to my students. For instance, I purposely did not say, "That looks like a California tan, Honorée." An apparently innocent remark, it suggests the speaker has held in mind an image of Honorée sunbathing.

One can be personal in one's relationship with a student and nevertheless maintain one's professional integrity. I share my colleagues' wariness of the personal. Many of our students are extremely attractive persons. They've reached a stage of ideal physical development, and they're determined to appear attractive to each other. I believe that most of us faculty members strive successfully to remain unaffected by the carnal dimension of their lives.

I suppose that in its race toward destruction, the human species is breeding itself toward greater and greater heights of physical beauty. Among college students, attractive males and females are likely to locate each other, to mate, and to produce children who are even more attractive than their parents. And so on.

Honorée Evans would be my nominee as the exemplary female to demonstrate a survival-of-the-beautiful theory. Her face is not remarkable—her eyes are a little too small for that—but it is classically "pretty." While her skin is neither pale nor dark, it's clear and rosy, and in the sun it apparently browns very sweetly.

Honorée is a standard height, not thin and not heavy. The parts of her body are correctly proportioned, even her hands and fingers. When she puts her hair up, one savors the revelation of each of her ears.

One imagines that her parents are handsome creatures, who were approaching but not actually achieving physical perfection until they produced this dazzling daughter. Here at the university, I'm certain Honorée is destined to find a tall, blond young man, marry him, and produce a child who will advance the beauty of the species that much further. By then, however, I shall be dead or at the very least mercifully have lost my vision.

Some time ago, in this very same course, Modern Short Fiction—which I've taught for at least twenty years and which enrolls students from every college of the university—I had an unremarkable student, one Jennifer Talley. One morning, late in the spring semester, this student came to class in a tailored navy suit, a ruffled ivory silk blouse, high heels and stockings. She'd washed and brushed her hair so that it was like some exquisite light-brown treasure around her face, and she'd applied make-up so that her best features—large blue eyes and a mouth of surpassing elegance—were now very much in evidence.

I've surmised that Jennifer had dressed up for a job interview that day. What I can't account for is that her classmates took no note of her appearance.

Decorum is important to me, and I'm certain I maintained mine that morning, but I felt as if some willowy goddess had dropped from the heavens into my classroom. I lectured extremely well. When I glanced her way, Jennifer's face was so intensely alive that I could hardly stand to look at her, but I couldn't bear to look away for more than a moment or two.

This wasn't a schoolboy's crush. It wasn't even a grown man's folly. The training of my profession is to recognize and to honor beauty. Though I never saw her dressed up again, for me Jennifer Talley remained a radiant presence in my classroom until the end of the semester.

But when it came time to give Jennifer Talley a final grade, I had to face up to the fact that she deserved no higher than a B+. This saddened me. I took the grade to represent my own failure: either I had not discerned the virtue in her work, or else as her teacher, I had not inspired the brilliance of which she was capable.

Venus had chosen to visit a mortal who had not apprehended her glory.

The following September, Venus had her revenge when I met Jennifer coming out of the campus bookstore, spoke to her most warmly, and received from her a truncated "Hi—" and a facial expression of unambiguous non-recognition.

Jennifer Talley affected my life a great deal while I hardly affected hers at all.

Our students come to us and depart with little notion of their incidental power over us. That young woman was probably delighted with her B+; it must have been well beyond her expectations. No doubt a teaching robot would have interested her every bit as much as I did.

But for a couple of months I had to live with my very soul shimmering from the effect of Jennifer Talley's one morning of dressing up before she came to my class.

If Jennifer had been profoundly affected by me—say, for instance, if I had explained something in a lecture that suddenly gave her a deep understanding of the fiction of Katherine Mansfield—then frequently thereafter she would have come to my office to discuss Mansfield and other writers. She would have changed her major to English and asked me to be her advisor. She would have asked me to write her recommenda-

tions for employment and for graduate school. After gradua-
tion, she would have expected me to correspond with her. I
would have been the one she asked to be the godfather of her
first-born child.

My point is that we teachers pay for the effect we have on
our students with a lifetime of responsible behavior toward
them. What do they pay for the effect they have on us?

Very well, I appreciate your patience. Back to the matter of
my behavior with Honorée Evans the day before Thanksgiving.

A week or two before, Honorée had come by to discuss the
possibility of becoming an English major. On that occasion I
was friendly and informative. I am a thorough advisor; from
memory I can recite our requirements for the English major,
and I can clearly explain them, a feat that has a humbling
effect on most students since even the brightest of them are
baffled by the language of academic documents.

I was able to be useful to Honorée in answering some questions she had about studying overseas—she plans to be in
France next year, I believe. Because she had come at a time
when I wasn't busy, I took the liberty of opening a casual
conversation. I asked her how she liked California.

Chit-chat, of course, is what I meant to indulge us both in, to
stretch the time out a bit. I've already described Honorée's
physical virtues. Though she's not a goddess, willowy or otherwise, she's certainly a pleasure to observe. She chooses her
clothes carefully and wears them neatly. Usually she puts her
hair up in an exactly crafted pony-tail; when she takes her
quizzes she has the endearing habit of grasping her bangs and
lightly yanking them as if to pull the answers up out of her brain
and wring them from her hair down onto the paper. Even her
handwriting has an exceptional flowing lucidity that makes it
stand out among the semi-literate scratchings of her peers.

"Together" is the term her peers use nowadays to describe someone like Honorée: she's a very together young woman. And yet on that occasion of her first visit to my office, Honorée—as her peers would put it—"lost it." She blurted out her story of a lout of a Rhode Island boyfriend who'd enrolled in the University of California at Santa Barbara purely for the beach culture, a boyfriend who'd sent her home early from her last visit to him, telling her she just didn't fit in with his friends.

Her story was not one that moved me particularly.

But I was moved by Honorée's revelation of her loneliness, which was of such a dimension as to cause her to speak intimately to a relative stranger across an abyss of more than forty years.

Because they always seem to be so intently *with* each other and to be so concerned with social matters, it's easy to forget the isolation in which many college students live. So far as I know Honorée is a young woman with friends of both sexes, she has as rich a social life as anyone could ask for, and yet in those moments of her telling me about her maggot of an ex-boyfriend, I came to understand that she is often in danger of being crushed by the weight of her loneliness.

Of course when she began crying, I stood up and came around my desk to her. It was perfectly natural—to both of us, I think—for her to stand up, too, and let me put my arms around her and pat her back and tell her that this cretin wasn't worthy of touching her little fingernail.

My wife tells me that I am not a man who easily demonstrates his affection. That seems to me a fair accusation. Even with my own daughters, now that they are grown, I find that I'm more inclined to shoulder-patting than to hugging. I wasn't comfortable standing in my office with my arms around Honorée Evans. I was aware of the door being open, and I'll admit that I kept my eyes on it and was immensely grateful that no one walked by during the minute or so that Honorée sobbed quietly against my chest.

My wife has also explained to me that physical contact can be healing. This was apparently the case with Honorée. In spite of my distraction and preoccupation with being seen by some passer-by, my embrace served to comfort her. She regained her poise. We released each other, smiled awkwardly, and returned to our chairs on the separate sides of my desk.

When I handed her a tissue from the box I keep in my desk drawer, Honorée blew her nose vigorously, then caught my eye and laughed out loud. I was amused, too, at how quickly our interview had changed from a tragedy to a comedy. We concluded with my encouraging her to pursue her plan to study overseas. Purposely I kept my seat when she stood up to leave. I did not wish her to feel that I would press her for further intimacy.

I wished no further intimacy with her.

The following Monday, in my mailbox in the department office, I received the note from Honorée that I have submitted to you. I took it at face value, as an expression of gratitude for the attention I had given her at a time when she desperately needed someone to listen to her. That it closes with the word "Love" did not seem to me then—and does not now seem to me—to mean anything other than Honorée's mild affection for me in the mood in which she composed her note. Otherwise, it has the tone and the formal qualities of an old-fashioned thank-you.

Here in the academy, we are not unlike the military in our attempts to codify every exchange between the members of our community. Of course our most intense scrutiny is focused on faculty-student relations. It is of utmost importance that the integrity of those relations be maintained. I believe that there should be, as there are in fact, rules against a professor's putting his arms around a student. And yet, on that occasion, it seems to me that my putting my arms around Honorée Evans was a necessary act, one that helped Honorée and, paradoxically enough, one that well served the university.

At my age, one becomes oddly prideful. I felt proud of myself for having chanced public censure in order to give comfort. I took into consideration that if Honorée had been a less attractive person, my response to her would not have been nearly as generous. Nevertheless, I knew that—at some personal risk—I had done the right thing.

I should have remembered how, in the grand sequence of human events, one decent act never stands alone. Send your brother the hundred dollars he wants to borrow now; next month he'll write to ask for a hundred more. Help an old lady cross the intersection only to find her collapsed in your arms and needing to be carried all the way home. Not that Honorée Evans came back to my office in need of another professorial embrace.

But, as I don't need to tell you, she did come back.

I am one of those professors who enjoys simply puttering around his office. Years ago I inherited my grandfather's leather-topped mahogany desk, the surface of which I keep clear of everything except my lamp. To make an informal conference area, I furnished the area in front of this desk with an oriental carpet and two comfortable chairs, one of them a rocker that is kind to my back. Tidying, filing, throwing away documents that have lost their relevance—there are always little tasks to be carried out in a room where one feels comfortable. And of course one has set aside articles and papers to be read on quiet afternoons.

Because I fought for it years ago, I am blessed with a corner office with a view of the lake as well as of the northern vista of our campus. It is tucked away in an obscure nook of the third floor; to find my office, you must round a sharp corner and pass through a narrow corridor.

On this particular afternoon, I had my office door closed, because I was listening, on my "boom box," as my wife and daughters like to call my portable stereo, to Horowitz's late recording of his own favorite solo piano pieces. The primary recreation of my recent years has been listening to classical music. Since my bad back required me to give up tennis, I've spent most of my free time reading about and listening to the great music of the eighteenth and nineteenth centuries.

With Horowitz and Mozart enhancing my vision, I was generally enthralled by my view down across the campus to our little city and Lake Champlain and the Adirondacks in the distance. I was standing at my west-facing window, with my attention completely given over to melody and harmony and the gulls riding the wind through the late fall sunlight, when I heard this soft knocking at my door.

When I opened it, there was Honorée—somewhat perplexed. "I didn't expect you to be here," she said, "but then I heard music. I just wanted to leave you this." From her book bag, she presented me with a bottle of Beaujolais Nouveau tied with a green ribbon and a small, ivory card. She wore her regular outdoor jacket but her skirt and shoes were dressier than what she usually wore to class.

I asked her in and closed the door behind her. If I am playing recordings in my office, I don't keep the door open. Closing it was perhaps not a prudent act; at the moment I thought only of not making a public nuisance with my music. As I took Honorée's jacket and hung it up, I did reconsider the issue of the closed door, but then she turned to me, rubbing her hands together, and said, "It's cozy in here. It feels great." I gave no further thought to opening the door and turning off the music.

To honor the bottle, I set it in the center of my desk, musing over the card—"to a really *decent* teacher". I thanked her for the wine, my fondness for which she must have learned about from some remark I made in class. I told her I was simply passing the time until late that evening when my wife would return from New Haven. Honorée told me she was simply passing the time until her parents flew into town the next morning to celebrate a Vermont Thanksgiving with her. I gestured toward the chairs in front of my desk. We sat down.

It was quite natural then to let the silence stretch between us while we listened to Horowitz play all the way through the Mozart Adagio in B Minor, a piece that I know so well I have even dreamed of playing it, though I am no musician. At its conclusion I said, "You know, Honorée, my wife accuses me of trying to dress like this gentleman." I showed her the CD cover's picture of Horowitz in his bow tie and matching breast-pocket handkerchief. Laughing politely, Honorée said that my wife was right and that the resemblance wasn't merely in the way we dressed.

For that observation I thanked her. I confessed to her that I had always secretly fancied that I looked a bit like the famous pianist. I had even fancied that in my own fashion I am devoted to the esthetic life with something resembling Horowitz's integrity. I surprised myself by revealing these notions to her.

"You know, Honorée," I told her, "I'll confess something else. I was shamefully glad that it turned out to be you at my door just now. With this music, this weather outside, and this light coming through my windows, there's almost no one I know who wouldn't have spoiled it. But you are exactly the person I should like to be sitting here at this moment."

She smiled and looked over her shoulder toward the window, near which a gull drifted on the wind. Then she blushed slightly and said, "What about your wife? Wouldn't you be glad to see her?"

"Oh, of course I would," I said. "But I wouldn't be shamefully glad. And I probably wouldn't invite her to sit down and listen to this music. We'd have things we knew we needed to do. So we'd leave right away to go home and prepare the house for our company tomorrow. Please don't misunderstand me, Honorée: I'm always glad to see my wife, but right now I'm glad to see you."

She was quiet a while, studying me. "I don't get it," she said.

"It's simple enough," I told her. "I hope you won't be offended by my telling you that literally *seeing you* is a great pleasure for me. It's also the case that you're someone whose thoughts and feelings I understand well enough to value."

Because I was so certain that my feelings about Honorée were decent and appropriate, I found myself struggling to articulate them. "You're a young person whose life—or what I know of it—appeals to me."

"You're sure you don't have a crush on me? It sounds sort of like that to me."

"Well, I guess it is sort of like that. But you're too young, or I'm too old. I think we just have to say that I appreciate you."

"You appreciate me." Honorée continued to study me, though now there was a softening to her face. "I thought that's what you did. That's why I brought you the present."

We turned our attention to the bottle of wine, standing alone on the maroon leather top of my desk. I guessed that because of the national insanity of our new drinking laws, she had had an older friend purchase it for her.

"I just thought of something, Honorée!" I rose from my chair and stepped to the corner behind my filing cabinet.

"Look what I have!" From the top of three cardboard cases, I plucked out two wine glasses. "These are from the days when we used to have sherry parties for our English majors," I told her. "Before they raised the drinking age. Back then I was always the one who made those arrangements. I have six dozen of these glasses packed away back here."

For my power to produce wine glasses, I was absurdly proud of myself, remembering the days when I had had to ask several of my colleagues not to refer to me, in the presence of students, as "Captain Sherry." I set the glasses on my desk on either side of the Beaujolais Nouveau.

"An opener?" she said very softly.

My pride vanished. "No," I said. "I don't think I ever had one of those. Sherry corks twist out."

With the sunlight shining directly in like that, my office had turned warm as an incubator. Horowitz had moved from Mozart to Schubert. My student and I sat and listened. The shaft of light slanting down from my window made the glasses sparkle and turned the wine translucent in its bottle. That half of my desk, bordered by shadow, looked like a painter's arrangement for a still-life.

Finally Honorée was the one to break the silence. "You're going to think I'm terrible."

"What?"

From her purse she extracted a corkscrew, one of those that folds up like a pocketknife.

"I'll swear to God, this is from my job last summer. I just remembered I had it," she said. "I waitressed at the Cape."

"Brilliant young woman!" I took the opener from her extended hand and stood up. The bottle gave me very little resistance. When I'd sniffed the cork, poured the wine, and handed her a glass, I lifted mine in a toast. "To bold resourcefulness!" I felt as if I'd accomplished something important. We drank.

"To appreciation," Honorée proposed.

"To a sublime afternoon," I offered.

Few segments of my life have been as pleasant as those long minutes I spent sitting with Honorée sipping the new Beaujolais in my warm office with the old master Horowitz playing Schubert and Liszt. The light outside began gradually deepening; the wind had calmed so that now the white gulls appeared suspended over the campus green.

"Do you know, Honorée, when I was your age, I never dreamed I would be the person I've become. I don't know exactly what I thought was going to happen to me, but I'm certain I never envisioned such luck as to be in the company of someone like you in my sixty-fourth year."

"You didn't?" Honorée stood up to examine a book on the shelf beside her, slipping off her sweater with her back to me. Her skirt was a Tartan kilt, and when she turned to drop the sweater in her chair, I saw that her white blouse had a pleated front.

"That's a very pretty blouse, Honorée. You know, the way you young women dress nowadays takes me back to my own days as a college student."

She turned to face me. "Yes, I've seen pictures of the styles back then. You like this?" She looked down the front of herself. "The other way I thought of wearing it was like this." She undid the button at her neck and the next one down, then pushed the garment back on her shoulders so that it opened as a frame around her collarbone. There was no hint of décolletage and nothing naughty about that arrangement of her blouse, but it was also, really, an artful presentation of that intricately molded triangle of Honorée's skin at the top of her chest.

As she looked to me for a response, I felt myself blushing a bit for the pleasure she offered me. "I must say," I said, "that wearing it like that makes a very pretty present of that little hollow at the base of your neck."

The seriousness with which Honorée studied my face reminded me that I had frequently noticed my students struggling to discern the levels of irony in my words. Was I mocking them or myself or fate?

"I don't mean to be inscrutable, Honorée. What I'm telling you is that your beauty is very powerful. Even this innocent place here." I touched my shirt just beneath my bow tie, smiled at her, and cleared my throat. "If I were on my death bed, breathing my last, and you walked into the room with your collar open like that, I'd make myself live another hour just for the sight of you."

She continued searching my face. Though I'd smiled at her to reinforce the honor and affection I intended to convey with my remarks, I became so undone by her seriousness that I felt my smile fading.

Honorée stood before me, our eyes locked. Master Horowitz approached the final notes of the Liszt sonata. I had no notion of what might be passing through her mind.

"Power," I said quietly. "All I mean to say is that you must be aware of your power."

Honorée was quiet a while longer. The recording ended, which seemed to change her mood. She crossed her arms in front of her; her expression was one of bemusement. "You think I don't know?"

I opened my arms and shrugged and smiled at her. "I don't know how you could know it," I said. "Only those of us who

are your witnesses can testify to the feelings you arouse in us."
My blush this time was for my phrasing, which I had not
intended to be so bold.

Now she smiled slightly. "You're sweet. You really are." She
turned toward my little compact-disc player. "I loved that music. Could you play it again?"

I bowed my head and reached to the black box to push the
play button. Horowitz began the Mozart once more.

When I turned my eyes back to Honorée, she had undone
the next button of her blouse and had her fingers on the one
after that. I inhaled so sharply that she heard me and smiled as
if to reassure me.

"Isn't this what you want?" She untucked the blouse from
her skirt. Her voice was soft, her expression kind.

I swallowed. My thoughts swirled like gulls blown up in a
sudden wind. "I hadn't thought of this," I whispered.

"But you had thought of it, Professor Riggins," Honorée
said, undoing her belt and quoting my phrasing from the
dialogues I often held with students in the classroom. "I'll bet
you're aware—" she was even imitating my voice—"that the
kind of power you're talking about is actually the power your
own desire has over you." In spite of her mocking me, her
voice kept its softness, its tone of almost familial teasing. She
unzipped and stepped out of her skirt.

I tried to keep my own voice level. "Honorée, I have no
desire to have sex with you."

"I know that."

I raised my eyebrows at her.

Keeping her eyes on me, she slipped off the blouse and stood
before me in her brassiere and half-slip.

"Just say 'stop' when you want me to stop." She reached
behind her and bent slightly forward.

I am not a man to whom a great many women have revealed their breasts. But even if I were—even if I personally had suckled at the breasts of Cleopatra, Helen of Troy, Jane Russell, and Kim Novak—I would not have been able at that moment to tell Honorée Evans, "Stop." In my own ethical evaluation of these events, I've realized that as I sat in my rocker gazing at Honorée, I was not rattled; on the contrary, I was planning to wait until I had seen all I wanted of her breasts and then to say, "Stop."

When she stood up straight and let her bra drop to the floor, I couldn't help inhaling sharply again. I raised my glass. "To your excellent health," I whispered. She nodded before she pushed the half slip down and stepped out of it. Then she picked up her glass and raised it in silence.

Leaning against my desk, she set the glass down and slipped off first one shoe, then the other. Dark blue tights covered her from her waist to her toes. With an arm across her stomach, she then propped up her other arm and hand to hold her wine glass just beneath her lips. The tone of her voice was as considerate as if I had been lying on my death bed. "This is not enough, is it, Professor Riggins?"

"No sex, Honorée." I used a stern tone.

She smiled and set her glass down. "No sex, Professor Riggins." Her voice hit the same notes mine had. "Definitely no sex." Sliding her tights and underpants down to the floor, she bent at the waist and presented me with the upside-down lightly muscled expanse of her back, the sight of which gave my own back a twinge. Straightening and stepping out of the wad of fabric at her feet, she became absolutely bare. Then, braced against my desk, she stood to face me with her hands on either side of her hips, palms flat against the leather surface.

"Your desk is nice," she murmured, looking down at it and

smoothing the leather with her hand, then glancing over at me. "I wonder why you keep it so clean?"

Until that moment, I had felt myself becoming so deeply anxious that I was on the verge of asking her please to put her clothes back on. But something about the circumstance and that question—which I'm certain Honorée intended only casually—had this extraordinary effect on me. Suddenly I felt my forehead relax, my worries dissolve. My temptation is to say that I wasn't myself, but my conscience instructs me to admit that I was as truly myself as I've ever been. I stood up, took my keys from my jacket pocket, and locked the door. "I've always thought that I might try it for a nap some afternoon," I told her, just about to take my seat again.

"Here. See if this will do for a pillow." I handed her the flat cushion from my rocking chair. "I want you to be comfortable."

Indeed the cushion worked very well for a pillow. Honorée lay back on the desk, stretched herself lengthwise, pulling the skin tight over her ribs and shrinking her waist outrageously. Then she settled her hands behind her head on the makeshift pillow, raised one knee, and studied the ceiling. "What is the name of this he's playing now?" she asked. "This is the part I liked before."

I sat down in the rocker and explained Mozart's chromatic harmonies in the B-Minor Adagio. Then I began telling her about Horowitz and his decision first to retreat from the public eye, then to return to performing. As I spoke, I confess that my eyes consumed Honorée whose every part, now that I could study her calmly, appeared tinted some slightly different shade of sun-tan or paleness. My voice took on a lilt, and the light in my office changed to deeper and deeper shades of gold.

Honorée shifted back to lying on her side, her knees bent and her body curled slightly toward me. As I spoke I found myself leaning closer and closer to her. She seemed to be listening intently. "What?" she asked me. "I can't quite hear you, you're speaking so softly," she said.

I cleared my throat. "I don't know why I'm talking this way," I told her in my normal voice. "Perhaps I'm trying to fit in with the music."

"It's fine with me," she said. "I just can't quite hear you."

And that is why I knelt at the desk, beside her face. To be able to speak softly to her and for her to be able to hear. To watch her face while I spoke. To hear her questions. Perhaps even to inhale her fragrance. But it was certainly not any sort of Satanic ritual. I had not hypnotized Honorée. I was merely teaching her some things I had learned over the years about music.

Of course I realize that it is reasonable to assume that either Honorée or I would have heard the custodian's footsteps or his keys jangling as he unlocked my door.

I realize that a more normal reaction on my part and on Honorée's would have been to rise, to move quickly, to try to shield her body from Mr. Lindberg's view and generally to disguise whatever it was that we were up to.

The only explanation I can offer is that Honorée and I were so intent on the subject matter I was conveying to her that we thought of nothing more than those words and the music we were hearing.

Yes, by that time the room was almost dark, though there was sufficient light. And yes, I was completely dressed, though probably Mr. Lindberg was not aware of what most—or at least a great many—people in this community know perfectly well, that while I am on the grounds of the university, I never remove my jacket and my tie. The suggestion that I was wearing some sort of costume is patently absurd.

Surely the facts that Honorée merely covered herself with

her hands and that I merely turned to the man and courteously asked him to leave indicate that whatever we were up to, we weren't feeling or acting particularly guilty.

You ask what we might have discussed that so held our attention. The year before he died, Horowitz granted an interview to the *New York Times*, in which he spoke of music's reassurance to the human body. He spoke of how our bodies are aware of time and of how that awareness produces a physiological anxiety. He said, "Music transforms time into a form of play for the body."

He said that music demonstrates for our bodies how the terrible punishment of our lives—mortality—is also the source of our deepest pleasure—music, art, love.

These were the things I whispered into Honorée's ear as she lay on my desk.

When Mr. Lindberg entered my office, Horowitz was about two-thirds of the way through Liszt's arrangement of the Schubert song "Ständchen." The one true regret I have about that afternoon is that Mr. Lindberg felt it necessary to empty my trashcan at that hour of the day.

From his opening my office door and entering until he backed out and closed the door behind him, Mr. Lindberg was in our presence for probably no more than forty-five seconds. At first, after he went away, Honorée and I made an effort to repair the mood he had damaged. In my attempt to recover my concentration, I had begun to explain to Honorée the technical problem of "Ständchen," the three-handed final variation. Very quietly she interrupted me by saying, "That man is calling the campus police right this minute."

"Yes, you're right," I said and rose and sat back down in my rocking chair. Apparently we both knew Mr. Lindberg was reporting us as certainly as we knew our own hearts were beating. I began to rock. Honorée pushed herself up to a sitting position and swung her feet around to the floor.

There have been few sadder moments in my life.

As the campus security report indicates, when the two officers arrived, my office door was open, Honorée was dressed and we were sitting on opposite sides of my desk, discussing the courses she might take in France next year. The wine was out of sight. There was no music.

We denied nothing and admitted nothing to the officers. But when they had left us alone, Honorée and I discussed this question thoroughly. We decided that denying the incident would draw more attention to it than admitting it.

I do not dispute what Mr. Lindberg says he saw, though his interpretation of the tableau was, as I hope I've explained to you, wildly incorrect.

I am grateful to the university for managing to keep the matter out of the newspapers and for holding this confidential hearing.

If the university had not decided to look into the matter, it's unlikely that I would have confided in my wife what transpired between Honorée and me. Marriage, even for the long married like Mrs. Riggins and myself, is fragile and complicated. But on the day I received the phone call from my chairman, I undertook to explain these events to my wife. As you can see, she has come with me to the hearing tonight, has been kind enough to support me in this public aspect of the incident.

But I'm certain she doesn't support my actions with Honorée. Her questions have been, "Why didn't you open the door when you thought of it? Why did you take out the wineglasses? Why didn't you say 'stop' when she gave you the chance to say it?" And who can deny the essential rightness of such questions?

I don't know why I didn't open the door, why I produced the

wineglasses, why I didn't say "stop," even as I'd so low-mindedly intended to, after having let my eyes have their fill of Honorée's breasts. According to the values by which I ordinarily live I should have taken these correct actions. I didn't.

Furthermore, I have little remorse about what I did and did not do. I'd certainly prefer for my wife not to have to undergo this humiliation. Had I been given a clear choice between my wife's humiliation and not having spent that time in my office with Honorée, I'd have chosen for my wife not to be humiliated.

I am voluntarily here before you tonight because I wish you to understand something essential: The man who chose what he chose that late sunny afternoon was not someone else. He is the same man who has honorably served this university for thirty-five years: the scholar, the teacher, the husband, the father, the citizen, the decent and decorous person whose deepest attention is ordinarily given to music and literature. He is also the man who did not discourage a female student from taking off her clothes for him.

Yes, Professor Schreckenberger, my sixty-fifth birthday will be coming up in May. How old is Honorée Evans? Well, I'm not certain, but it's most likely that she's nineteen. As you know, most college sophomores are eighteen or nineteen, and Honorée is more mature than most. But surely your question is more rhetorical than substantive, since you have already taken testimony from Honorée herself.

How do I feel about the difference in our ages in light of what happened? Please forgive me for saying so, Dean Poulin, but I believe the word I would choose is *immortal*. For a little while in the light of that room, I felt god-damned immortal.

And now if there are no more questions, Mrs. Riggins and I will be making our way home. I thank you for your patience with me this evening.

The Side Effects of Lucille

FROM THE FIRST CLASS she attended, Lucille Boudreau had my attention. There were nearly six feet of that woman, and her cinnamon-colored hair grew vigorously away from her head like some extraordinary bird's plumage. Expensive clothes hung on her body as if they understood the privilege she was giving them.

Ordinarily redheads didn't appeal to me. Ordinarily tall women were too gawky for my taste, but there was something sublime about Lucille. I imagined that she had never lived so much as one trashy minute.

When I invited her to my apartment for a drink after a Thursday afternoon class, I did so in innocence and despair. I was almost certain she would not accept. I thought—I think I even hoped—that a woman who wore a ring and who was that elegant would disdain the pleasures I meant my invitation to suggest to her. I knew little about her personal life except that she was commuting down from Montreal to take my poetry-writing workshop.

Lucille's skin smelled like a field of clover on a hot afternoon; it tasted faintly of bourbon.

In my bed, with the autumn twilight settling over our little northern city, she instructed me in such a manner as to bring her to a noisy orgasm. Then rather quickly she brought me to the same destination and rolled away, murmuring, "My husband will kill you first. He'll want me to witness that."

I have found that women making love with me for the first time often say startling things. I try to avoid responding to post-coital observations. Into the silence that I let fall around us, Lucille laughed and announced, "But I'm hungry. Let's go get something to eat before we have to start thinking about god-damn Carly."

At dinner she told me about god-damn Carly. Her husband was a Montreal thug who lived grandly. During the past couple of years, Carly Boudreau's lawyer had helped him beat charges of possessing drugs, selling drugs, and permanently disfiguring the face of a young woman who owed and hadn't paid Carly for drugs.

For the good of Lucille's poetry Carly let her drive across the border to take my writing workshop. Some years ago I won the Yale Prize with a book entitled *The Company of My Pleasure*. I no longer compose poems, but a few of my students have had significant literary careers. My reputation is that of an important enough teacher that even Carly Boudreau let his wife study with me.

Carly wanted Lucille to be known in Montreal as Carly Boudreau's wife the poet. He didn't mind if she stayed in

Burlington a few hours after class to shop or to have dinner. But Lucille said she'd be afraid to stay overnight unless she had an impeccable excuse.

On these trips, Carly didn't want to risk riding across the border with Lucille; he suspected the U.S. authorities might detain him for questioning.

"He can get down here any time he wants to," Lucille told me over Veal Francis at Vermont Pasta. "But he doesn't like to take chances just for a pleasure trip."

I reached across the table for her freckled hand. "Lucille, why did you go to bed with me? Why did you bring me into this?"

The focus of her green eyes was like heat on my face. "I didn't *go* to bed; I *came* to bed with you." Her voice was level. "And I didn't *bring* you into this; I let you into a place you seemed most eager to enter."

I was quiet. Lucille smiled down at her plate before she continued. "You know in *The Godfather* how they gun some-body down in a restaurant?" Her eyes widened, and her voice was low. "I'm sitting here thinking how Carly could have that done to us." She tapped her plate with her fork and watched my face. "This tastes better than it would if I were thinking something else," she said. Then she put her head back and laughed. People in the restaurant turned to stare.

Lucille was wearing a cream-colored silk blouse and a dark green double-breasted jacket with big shoulder-pads. As if it carried some wattage of electrical current, her mane of wiry, reddish hair stood out from her head. Studying her flushed face, I remembered from that afternoon that her underwear was a matched set of extravagant white silk with cream lace.

Mrs. Carly Boudreau was a visual treasure.

Not without ability as a poet, she was laughably cautious in her technique and timid in her subject matter. After the next

Tuesday afternoon's class, as we were settling into my bed, I pointed out this paradox to her. "You know, in person you are very bold," I told her. "Why, then, don't you take a similar attitude with your poetry? Why are you writing cramped little stanzas about flower arrangements that wilt on your dining room table?"

Magnificently Lucille rose from my bed, the jouncing of her breasts sufficient to stop my heart as she kicked through the pile of her clothes to locate her underpants. My apologies neither slowed her dressing nor prevented her from jerking her comb through her hair and stalking out of my apartment leaving the air crackling.

Slowly putting my own clothes back on in my empty apartment, I swore to save my criticism for the classroom. It was when I turned to straighten the covers on my bed that it occurred to me how, in such anger, Lucille might dispatch goddamn Carly to Burlington to discuss poetry—and related matters—with me. To consider how seriously I should take the threat of Carly Boudreau, I had to lie down awhile.

But in Thursday's class, in a yellow blouse that flamed like the maple leaves outside on the campus green, Lucille sat in her customary seat at the seminar table. A sheaf of poems lay significantly in front of her. During this workshop Lucille addressed generous remarks to her fellow students, but she hardly turned her face toward me. I didn't try to elicit a response from her. The secret of my teaching has been to say as little as possible, thereby letting the students teach themselves and each other.

After class, without a word or even a direct glance, she left her poems with me. The small handwritten note attached to them read, "When you've had a chance to read these, I'd like to meet with you in your office to discuss them."

The poems were a breakthrough for Lucille; they were also fascinating as what I have privately come to think of as "life documents."

The first described the vast plain of Laurentian valley farmland during a blizzard on a January night and ended with the speaker's consciousness suddenly spiraling upward beyond the clouds into the stars.

Another gave an account of a country girl coming to Montreal, finding work, taking a boarding-house room, and settling into her rented bed that first night beneath an eiderdown that held the smell of a hundred other immigrants to the city.

The third told of waiting outside a door behind which the speaker suspected someone was being murdered; her fear and anger and helplessness became excruciating by the poem's end.

When Lucille appeared at my office before class the following Tuesday, her wide-brimmed hat was tilted forward so severely that I could barely see her eyes. She wore a navy-blue pinstripe suit, a navy silk shirt, and a thin white tie.

With my finger I tapped her poems on the desk in front of me and nodded my head.

"I thought so," she said. "I'm sorry I acted so childishly last week. You're a great teacher. You knew what to say to make me discover what I really wanted to write."

Her response was not so very exceptional. I've found that most writing students wish a simple yes or no from their teachers.

After a pause, in which Lucille seemed to be searching for something in my face, she went on. "I have an idea for thanking you," she said. She would not explain what she had in mind. Nor would she agree to come back to my apartment that afternoon.

Perhaps I should have been suspicious of her. Perhaps I was.

But I was going through a phase in which there were few women in my life. The long hours I spent in my empty apartment so deeply oppressed me that I was willing to risk some harm in exchange for Lucille's company.

After Thursday's class she drove me back to my place and helped me pack my suitcase for a weekend holiday. When we went back out to the street, a black-windowed white limousine was waiting for us outside my apartment building. Apparently Lucille's luggage had already been stowed away in the huge car's trunk.

From where we sat in the rear seat, our young driver was far away. Gliding smoothly out of town and onto the interstate in that car was like traveling through space. Lucille arranged my seat so that I was deeply reclining, then signaled the driver to turn on the sound system—a recording I had mentioned being fond of in class some days ago, The Guarneri playing the second of the late Beethoven Quartets.

She opened and poured us glasses of a chilled bottle of Mosel.

While the car sped through the central Vermont river valley, Lucille thinly sliced a gold and brown mottled pear, feeding these slices first to me and then to herself. Finally, she removed her jacket, knelt on the carpeted floor in front of me, removed her blouse, peeled her slip down to her waist, anointed her lightly freckled breasts with drops of wine, then raised herself over me to offer her sweetened nipples to my mouth.

In the limousine, moving above me, peering down into my face, Lucille made a low humming in her throat. "I've read your poems," she said. "I know what you want. I know exactly what you want," she whispered, lightly brushing my cheek with her breast.

She drew away from me and began dressing as our driver brought us into a town that I recognized. He delivered us to the Pickering Inn and set out our luggage. Lucille dismissed him with instructions to pick us up on Monday morning.

Inside, at the desk, Lucille stepped up to the desk, signed us in as Mr. and Mrs. E. A. Robinson, and asked if she might pay in advance. When the clerk had calculated our bill—a little too quickly, I thought—she paid him in cash.

High-ceilinged and spacious, our bedroom had a fireplace and one entire wall of glass mirrored by the darkness outside. While Lucille ordered food to be brought to our room, the bell boy laid kindling and paper to start a fire, accepted my tip, then bowed out of the room. Soon came a rolling table offering bread, butter, paté, cheese, and fresh raspberries, with a separate tray holding tall wine glasses and a bottle of Château Yquem in a crystal basket of ice.

Lucille drew a bath, helped me undress, then while I soaked in the huge tub, she undressed herself and rolled the table of food into the bathroom. From the tub, we picked food from the tray and ate with our fingers, and when we'd had our fill of it, Lucille shampooed and rinsed my hair. She took her time toweling both of us dry.

Arm in arm we walked to the enormous bed. I lay naked and staring across the room toward the fireplace flames, while Lucille opened and poured the wine. She stood beside the bed, arching her back as if to correct some slight stiffness. The firelight gleamed on her freckled skin.

I lifted my glass: "To the next great poet of Montreal!"

Lucille chuckled. "Whoever that may be," she murmured.

Just as her glass touched her lips, it slipped from her fingers and fell onto the carpet. "Oh," she said. Her arms flapped loosely to her sides. When she looked down at the spilled wine, her body took a slight lurch forward, as if she were about to pitch down onto her face. But she caught herself and remained standing, though swaying.

Then I was beside her. I held her and helped her lie down on the bed. My hands touching her skin felt something drastically changed in her body.

"What's wrong, Lucille? Can you tell me what's wrong?"

She didn't answer. I was so ashamed of how frightened my voice sounded that I swore to shut up and keep my wits about me.

Pulling bedcovers over Lucille, I saw that she had grasped the notepad from beside the telephone, but when I started to take it from her, she wouldn't let go. She had strength in that hand, though her body had become as sluggish as an about-to-pass-out drunk's. Even her face was slack, but her eyes were open and apparently alert. Those eyes watched my face as I arranged the pillows under her head.

She glanced over at the table and back again to my face. There was a pen there. It occurred to me that perhaps she meant to write me a note. I put the pen into her hand and fixed it in her fingers, her eyes seeming to tell me that I was acting correctly. But I had to help her move her pad-holding hand and her pen-holding hand together, had in fact to move the pen-point to the exact place on the paper where she might begin the note.

Her face distorting with the effort, Lucille tried to put words onto the notepad. She couldn't. After long minutes, she had made only a skewed letter S. About to scream with frustration, I was on the verge of instructing her to please stop this hopeless project, when I realized that actually what she had managed to set down was the number five. I said it aloud. Her eyes met mine; her face relaxed. We continued staring at each other.

Somehow she was making me come to know something.

"Two," I said.

Lucille closed her eyes.

"Three."

Her eyes stayed shut.

"One," I said, and her eyes immediately opened.

"Five, one," I said. She continued to gaze at me, then glanced down at the pad and pen. I took them from her, put my one beside her five and showed it to her. "Four," I said. Her eyes told me I was right, and I wrote it down. Now I knew what she was trying to do. Five-one-four was the Montreal area code. By guessing each digit of it and watching her eyes, I got down a phone number, though the project took us almost a quarter of an hour.

All this while, I was having difficulty keeping my emotions under control. I couldn't get rid of the thought that if she died there, I would be held responsible, if not by the law, then certainly by Carly Boudreau.

With her watching my face, I stared at the number I'd written on the pad. "Lucille, is this Carly's number?"

She closed her eyes.

"Is it a friend of yours?"

She kept them closed.

Panic was rising in me. "Jesus Christ, Lucille!" I shouted, knowing even before my vocal cords stopped vibrating that it was idiotic to yell at the woman for what had befallen her. Her eyes were on me.

"I'm sorry," I said and leaned forward and kissed her temple. "My dates don't usually turn out like this," I murmured to her as I picked up the phone to dial the number in Montreal. She kept watching me.

"Hello?" This was a woman's voice.

"Hello," I blurted before realizing that I hadn't thought of what to say. Something instructed me to speak with caution. "Ah, I uh . . . ,"

"Yes?"

"I have a medical problem here. I wonder if there's someone there who might help me?"

"May I ask who's calling?"

"I, uh—. I'm calling for a friend of mine. Someone who's too sick to come to the phone."

There was a blur of noise on the other end of the line, as if the woman had covered the receiver with her hand and was telling someone what I'd said. Then the woman's voice came back: "May I ask why you've called this number?"

Lucille watched me intently.

"My friend—ah, my friend wrote down this telephone number."

"He wrote it down?"

"It's a she," I said, wondering if I had to say that. "She's unable to talk."

The woman's hand went over the receiver again, then rather quickly there was another voice on the line, a man's this time. "Hello, this is Dr. Vogan. With whom am I speaking?"

"Hello, Dr. Vogan." Lucille's face relaxed when she heard me say that name. "Dr. Vogan, I'm calling on behalf of Lucille Boudreau. She seems to have had a seizure of some kind. She managed to give me your telephone number."

"From where are you calling, sir?"

"We're in the States, Dr. Vogan."

"And what is your name?"

"I'd rather not say, sir."

"But you are a friend of Lucille Boudreau's?"

"Yes sir."

"And Mrs. Boudreau, I gather, has collapsed?"

"Yes sir."

"Her body is limp, and she can't speak, but her face registers consciousness?"

"Yes sir."

"Well, I guess you're about to find out just how close a friend of Lucille Boudreau's you are. She has Padgett's Syndrome. It's very rare. Fewer than a hundred cases in North America have been diagnosed. It doesn't even affect its victims very often—maybe four or five times during a normal lifespan. What it does is exactly what you're seeing in Mrs. Boudreau."

"What should I do for her? Should I bring her there to you for treatment? Should I take her to the hospital in—" I stopped myself.

"If you're able to take care of her where you are, then you should remain there. If you're not, then you should take her home or to a hospital. There is no treatment for a Padgett's Syndrome seizure. It will last at least twenty-four hours and probably no longer than three or four days. The patient needs to be kept comfortable. She can sip liquids. Her body will continue to function, though it'll be slowed down a great deal. Keep her warm. Don't let her become dehydrated. Help her to the bathroom as often as necessary. See that she doesn't lie or sit in the same position for more than an hour or so at a time, unless she's sleeping."

Surprisingly enough then, Doctor Vogan chuckled.

"Sir?" I said.

"I'm sorry. I just remembered that the main complaint of patients undergoing Padgett's Syndrome seizures is that they're extremely bored. So far as we know, their mental processes are unaffected by the seizure. Some have even described experiencing unusual mental alertness. Which means, I suppose, that if you can manage it, you should try to keep Mrs.

Boudreau entertained. At any rate, if you need further advice, here are some phone numbers where I can be reached." Dr. Vogan gave me two more numbers, I thanked him, and we said goodbye.

"He says I'm supposed to entertain you." Lucille's eyes widened a bit. I thought I even saw her mouth suggesting a smile. I stood up beside the bed and recited for her some lines of e e cummings:

> *anyone lived in a pretty how town*
> *with up so floating many bells down*

I know a good many poems by heart, which impresses most of my students, and because it goes over well in the classroom, I've learned to recite with a fair amount of expressiveness. Performing for Lucille, I found that I felt absurdly proud when her face appeared to register pleasure. Then her eyes were blinking.

"Water?"

Her eyes closed.

"Bathroom?"

She looked straight at me.

"One bathroom escort coming right up." I forced good cheer into my voice. With a flourish, I pulled the bedcovers away from her. The sudden sight of Lucille's inert body provoked some feeling in me that I couldn't really comprehend—not revulsion, not attraction, but something close to curiosity.

"Here we go," I said, putting an arm under her knees and another behind her back. Her arm fell across my shoulder. She could grasp me slightly to hold herself up. I carried her into the bathroom and sat her down on the commode. Then I stood beside her with my hands on her shoulders to help steady her.

While she sat there, I became aware of the surrealism of my

standing naked beside her, propping her up on that fancy commode. I was staring down the front of Lucille's slightly bent-forward body. Her breasts splayed slightly outward, and her belly ballooned out a bit. Then her long thighs angled inward toward her knees, but her shins and heels tilted outward, with the toes of her feet turned in toward each other on either side of the commode.

My view of Lucille was stunningly anti-erotic.

But then her head bent forward a little more so that her hair fell over her breasts. Something about that sight—a swatch of cinnamon-colored hair across a pale curve of breast—instigated a segment of my sexual chemistry. Looking downward as I was, I actually remarked my cock's twitching outward ever so slightly. To this inane gristle, I made a mental speech about the failures of a biology so imprecise in its sexual coding.

Finally Lucille urinated. My assumption was that her sphincter had had to overcome her awareness of my being right there beside her. When she finished, I took a breath and bent over her to pluck off a length of toilet paper.

I remembered a Yeats poem I would try to recite for her at a suitable time.

"Ready for the trek back, Lucille?" I was beginning to sound like Nurse Ratchett. I squatted beside her to pull her arm around my shoulder, then I helped her stand. Together we wobbled back into the bedroom. With me, at that moment, Lucille must have been wondering how long her seizure would hold us hostage.

But it wasn't a negative experience to be able to lower her gently down to the bed, swing her legs around and up onto the bed, pull the covers up over her, and tuck her in. It felt all right to serve her like that.

We stared at each other until I reached for my glass of the

Chateau Yquem. When I'd taken a pretty hefty swallow, I noticed Lucille's eyes on the glass.

"Jesus, excuse me, Lucille. I'm a pig. You're not the first woman to remark it. Here, let me help you." I lifted her head for her to have a sip of it. "Enough? No? Well, OK, let's have another go at it."

Maybe if my body were gorked out with a Padgett's Syndrome seizure, I'd figure I might as well treat it to a sizable dose of Chateau Yquem. I sympathized with Lucille enough to give her as much wine as she seemed to want. After a short time of the two of us using the same glass, we'd almost emptied the bottle.

"Well now," I said, setting our glass on the bedside table. "Let me look into your eyes, my dear, and see what intricate patterns of thought and feeling I can discern."

Lucille's green irises were flecked with gray. The more I studied them, the less I was able to differentiate between what was green and what was gray. Staring into those eyes, I started wanting some access to Lucille's interior life. I leaned closer. I touched my lips to hers.

What I had in mind was just an affectionate brushing of her mouth—your basic peck-on-the-run. I was perfectly aware that she had only about fifteen percent control over her facial muscles.

But here is the thing: there was a buzz to that numbed-out kiss. Something was there that made me go further than just an Aunt-Susie-brush-of-the-lips.

Then I backed away from what seemed to be happening and took another look into Lucille's eyes. Here, too, the phenomenon was enigmatic, but it seemed to me to be weighted toward the encouragement side of the scale.

While I was kissing her again, I tried to search my conscience. Admittedly it wasn't the ideal circumstance for soul examination; on the other hand I actually had to be doing something with Louise before I could make a judgment about whether or not it was a thing she wanted to be doing. So as I was kissing her, I really did try to determine if kissing was what she wanted to be doing.

When I looked at her face, her eyelids were hooded, neither open nor closed.

There's a question, I suppose, as to how sober I was in these moments of deliberation and passion.

Nevertheless, my considered opinion was—is—that Lucille wanted that kiss.

And more.

I can swear that Lucille's nipples were erect. She was one of those women whose nipple-definition was usually very low. From what past experience I'd had with her, I knew that it took a high level of arousal to provoke such tumescence of her nipples.

Could her body act independent of her mind in this situation?

"Lucille, is this what you want?" I whispered to her as I nuzzled my way down her belly.

Peering down at me, her eyes were open. Then they were closed. Then they were open again. But I felt this energy moving through her skin.

And she was wet before I ever touched her there with my tongue.

Even as I went on and on with my attentions to Lucille, I was thinking about the testimony of rapists, which I've never studied but which I'm certain must include such remarks as "There was no doubt in my mind that she wanted it" and "How can you say that it was against her will if she was wet before I ever touched her?"

These negative considerations did not stop me.

The excitement I felt might have been heightened by the philosophical dimension I brought to the tactile experience.

When I came, I was looking Lucille straight in the eyes, something I realized in that moment that I'd never done before with any woman. My orgasms have always so embarrassed me that I haven't wanted to be seen.

So far as I know Lucille did not come.

I think I would have known.

"Lucille, I'm sorry," I heard myself whispering as I drew away. "I hope that wasn't something you didn't want to happen."

Her eyes were open, observing me intently. Then they were closed.

I lay staring at the ceiling, considering the ambivalence of every sexual encounter. Always there is a voice saying, *I don't want this,* perfectly harmonizing with the voice that sings, *I want this, I want this!* Is it not, then, eternally a question of which is the louder voice?

When I woke, the wall of glass had turned into a wall-sized window that looked out on sky and trees. Careful not to wake Lucille, I eased out of bed, still naked, and tip-toed over to have a look.

Outside, in a small forest glade, under a stormy sky, were a fawn, standing still but with its ears twitching, and a large brown rabbit, moving slowly as it nibbled at something on the ground. The two creatures seemed unaware of each other, though they were not more than six feet apart.

I shifted my eyes upward slightly and saw what I was surprised not to have seen first, two large crows perched in the hemlock branches around the glade, bobbing their heads as if they were the audience for the rabbit and the little deer.

The knock on the door was the maids—a couple of high school girls, really—wondering when we wanted them to do our room. I asked them to do it now, while the lady was taking her bath. I told them we could let the bathroom go without cleaning a day, but we'd really appreciate it if they'd make up the bed with fresh sheets.

Back in the bathroom with Lucille, I very gingerly washed her face and ears with the washcloth. "Got to do the lady's hands, too," I told her. I took a long time to massage each finger, each little web between her fingers.

When I'd let the water out of the tub and engineered Lucille up and into a sitting position on the commode, wrapped in a huge brown towel, I was able to use the blow-dryer on her hair. The result was a much less dramatic-looking Lucille than the one who'd attended my classes and the one who'd checked into this room with me. With its strands no longer separated and teased out, her hair was a darker shade of red. It had lost that wiriness that made it stand out from her head. Now it hung straight as a schoolgirl's.

Without make-up, too, Lucille's face had a plain sweetness to it that seemed to me almost another dimension of her personality. This must have been the freckle-faced young woman who years ago had come off a prairie farm into the city of Montreal to look for a job.

I checked to see that the maids had finished and left the bedroom. Then, with her towel still wrapped around her, I sat Lucille in a chair by the window while I rummaged in her suitcase. There I found a long green silk nightgown and a black silk robe, which I brought to her, one in each hand. She gave me her open-eyed approval of my choices.

I dressed her carefully and used pillows from the bed to arrange her in her chair. So that we could both look out on the small forest glade, I moved a chair for me beside hers. From room service I ordered breakfast for us. Using our eyes-closed-or-open code, I learned that she liked cream but no sugar in her coffee. I gave her sips as she seemed to want them.

Through the late morning and early afternoon, Lucille and I sat by the window, watching the stormy weather have its way with the trees, watching the bluish-grey clouds sail across the horizon. I hoped we might see the rabbit or the deer return to the glade beneath our window.

I was quiet the whole time, attentive to Lucille, ready to respond to the slightest signal from her. I think I expected the seizure to begin releasing her, but the longer we stayed there, the more inert she seemed to become.

She generated no wish, no signal of any sort, while I became more and more receptive. I was a radio tuned to a station that had gone off the air.

My single desire was for Lucille to come back.

The phone rang. When I answered it, a man's voice said my name.

"Yes?" I said.

"Carly Boudreau here."

Instantly my sense of self returned to me, along with some fast calculating about Carly Boudreau. The receiver felt slick and hot in my hand. If god-damn Carly had managed to trace me to this room, then I knew I had to take him seriously. Even if he was the grossest amateur of a thug, he would have no difficulty dispatching me.

"Professor, we'd like you to prepare to depart the inn. We have a ride waiting for you. We'll give you a quarter of an hour to pack your things. Then we'd like you to bring your luggage and meet us out here in the lobby."

I checked my watch. "What about—?"

"Mrs. Boudreau should remain in the room."

Momentarily, I wondered if informing Carly of Lucille's condition would make any difference in how he treated me. I decided it wouldn't.

"All right," I said.

At the other end, the line went dead.

I dressed and packed, of course. I didn't talk with Lucille, because I was embarrassed at how I was sweating and how my fingers were trembling. Some of the time I was walking around in that room, I was sobbing out loud. I didn't want to die for what I had done, and I couldn't help imagining certain ways that Carly Boudreau might have me killed.

My preparations took only eight or nine minutes. I set my bag at the door and walked back toward the wall of glass. In spite of my panic, I approached Lucille slowly.

She had not moved; I was certain of that, though I had not been able to make myself look directly at her until now. Her eyes were open, watching me. The window's afternoon light gave a sheen to her black gown and her deep red hair. From her face every line of age or worry had disappeared. Her eyes widened in a look that was joyful or sorrowful, I didn't know which.

I knelt in front of her and managed to look directly into those green-gray eyes for a moment. They held such an intensity of life that I was forced to envision myself getting shotgunned down in the lobby. Sobbing again, distracted, I picked up Lucille's hand and put my lips to her fingers. "I wish you could help me," I said, "but I know you can't."

To my credit, I regained my composure before I left the room. Reaching back to pull the door shut behind me, I noticed Lucille's silhouette against the window with only the smooth curve of her hair catching the light.

Seeing her like that seemed to calm me. Instead of a deeper

fear, as I walked down the corridor, an odd notion came to me. If Carly left her alone and Lucille remained where she was, the room's next occupants would marvel over her, tip-toeing up to her and touching her face.

By the time I reached the lobby, my anxiety had changed to curiosity as to how Carly would go about exacting his revenge.

It was the cocktail hour. A number of guests were sitting and standing all through that spacious area. Two well-dressed, middle-aged men sat some distance from each other, legs crossed, reading newspapers. I thought that whichever of them cast his eyes up for a look at me was likely to be Carly Boudreau. I expected first the look and the nod of recognition, then the shotgun blast. But as I walked toward the exit, not a single person took note of me.

The only noise was the guests' mild chatter.

At the door, I was greeted by the same blond young man who some hours previously had chauffeured me to this place. He smiled faintly as he took my bag and held open the door of his vehicle. No one was inside waiting for me, but even after I had been closed into the empty compartment, I anticipated a shot or an explosion.

There was only the quiet and the scent of leather.

The chauffeur entered the distant front seat and began driving out of town.

When we reached the interstate, music came on the car's stereo system, The Guarneri again playing one of the late Beethoven quartets. I wondered if god-damn Carly had given the driver instructions to play the same music for me that I had heard in Lucille's company.

I could have switched on the intercom and questioned the driver, but I decided I didn't really want to know why he was playing that music. With the intention of trying simply to enjoy the sonorous tones of the composition, I settled back into my seat. It was twilight. The limousine was gliding through a river valley with dark mountains rising on both sides of the highway, and I was alive when I might have been dead. My mood could hardly have been more exactly attuned for hearing the last Beethoven string quartet.

But here is the thing. I was put off by the music. The Guarneri whined; the sounds it made grated my feelings. The adagio passage that I had trained myself to love now made me frantic. Finally I had to switch on the intercom to ask the driver to turn off the music.

The limousine delivered me back to my apartment. Through the rest of the weekend, I was cautious enough to stay indoors, and of course I did not answer the phone. But I went grocery shopping on Monday, and on Tuesday I taught my classes as usual. Several students in the writing workshop commented on Lucille's absence, though no one directly asked me about her.

To my colleagues and students, my life must appear to be proceeding according to its usual patterns. But that musical unpleasantness in the limousine was the first symptom of a much larger misfortune. Music, food, books, movies that should give me pleasure have now become abrasive occasions.

Until one is denied them, one doesn't realize how much one's days are structured around the small delights one has cultivated over the years. I find it impossible to enjoy an evening out with the dependable women who in the past have escorted me through hard times. If I meet a new woman, no matter how attractive she is, I find it impossible to sustain my desire for her even for the length of time it might take to consummate my interest.

Pleasurable experience is no longer possible for me, though

it seems everywhere available to others far less capable of appreciating it than I.

Apparently, the best I can hope for is a life of neutral sensation.

Constantly I work at retraining my mind not to seek out its customary pleasure-giving memories. But of course I can't avoid giving detailed consideration to my encounter with Lucille. I am more than a little bitter. Even though my affliction is not visible, my suffering is hellish.

But since I am not actually ill, I have little hope of ever being cured.

Again and again I am led back to my memory of Lucille sitting by the window in her black robe. How still she sat as I approached her for the last time! How her eyes blazed!

Trouble at the Home Office

LET ME BE STRAIGHTFORWARD. I was seeing some-body, and Susan found out. With the afternoon sunlight streaming through our living room windows, she and I had a quiet but definitely unpleasant chat.

Peter, she said with her lips tightening. I know these things happen. But I'm not just going to stand by. You make your choice. Either you're in or you're out.

We've got two kids. We agreed that I would cease seeing somebody. As of immediately. The hard line, though not un-reasonable. I chose in.

But somebody had some things to say—or to shout about in my office. Why wasn't she asked what she wanted and who the hell ordained my wife as the one to say when she and I were finished? Look at *her*, was she dirt, was she compost for the garden of my marriage? Look her in the eyes, damn it, wasn't I man enough at least to do that?

This was Julie Munroe, from Sports Spot, where I worked. I was Public Relations and Advertising. Julie was our Senior Fitness Instructor. Compact, with long dark hair and delicate features, Julie had a physique that made our members—male and female—blink the first time they saw her in her leotard. Julie disconcerted people; she was small and had this girlish face, but she was the fittest person I ever met. And she took no shit.

My situation was impossible. I had a talk with the boss.

Ben Fulton and I went way back to when I came off the tour and he was looking for a tennis instructor who could attract new members to Sports Spot. In 1975 I beat Nastase in the quarterfinals at Bretton Woods. Doodly-squat on the tour, but for a few years around here that credential helped make me the pro every tennis-playing housewife wanted lessons from. They signed their kids up, too.

Teaching was easy for me, easier than playing had been, and they used to say I had a natural gift and a perfect body for the game. So in those early days I had helped make Sports Spot successful, and in the last few years Sports Spot had made Ben Fulton a wealthy man.

Do you want me to fire her? he asked.

I told him no, she'd have us in court and in the papers, not to mention beating the crap out of both of us.

She could do it. He shrugged and grinned. Then he said, tell me about her, Peter.

I can't do that, Ben, I said. But I did go ahead and share a thought or two with him about Julie, because over the years Ben has been generous with me. He gave me my own office, he looked the other way when my clients needed individual conferences, and when I burned out on teaching tennis, he let me move up to management.

She's even better than she looks like she would be, Ben, I said. She has the power, I whispered.

He nodded and gazed out his window. We were quiet for a while.

So what Ben and I worked out was that with a fax machine and a computer, there was no reason why most of the time I couldn't work at home. No reason to come into Sports Spot if my being there was going to cause a disruption.

What we said officially was that I was being given a leave of absence. This had the appearance of punishment. It calmed Julie and the other female fitness instructors who sympathized with her. A certain calming effect, Ben said on the phone and chuckled. Not too much action around here without you, Peter.

That's how we like it, isn't it, Ben, I said. I wasn't kidding. There comes a time when you want to give up all the bullshit that goes with fooling around, but I kept that to myself. Quiet around here, too, I told him, and my work is good, don't you think, Ben?

It's great, Peter, Ben said. At the edge of his voice I could hear what he wasn't saying. He had little respect for my ideas; he revised all my press releases before they went out. He was polite about it, but basically I was just the guy who produced his first drafts.

Nevertheless, there I was, set up at home on the third floor. A few years ago Susan and I had had half of the attic finished, thinking we might want to rent a room to a college student. Then Susan's grandfather died, leaving her enough money to keep us from really needing rental income. When I told her I was going to start working at home, Susan was delighted that we'd finally be able to put that room to use.

It had shelves and a skylight. Instead of a new floor, we had just put down some old carpet from our bedroom. I had to buy a desk and some chairs, but Ben insisted on Sports Spot's paying for my computer and fax machine.

Maybe I wasn't an advertising genius, but brilliance wasn't what Sports Spot needed, just somebody to keep the public informed. I understood how to do that, maybe even better than Ben did.

I've never had what coaches call "a work ethic," but I put in my hours; I put forth some effort. If I didn't give the job my all, at least I gave it my most.

And things around home were better than they had been for awhile. With Julie off my mind, I was able to focus my attention on Susan. As her anger subsided, I began remembering what an attractive person I married. She's blond, tall, very thin and willowy. Suddenly I noticed what subtle taste in clothes she had, what a pleasure she was to look at. You might say that I revitalized my interest in Susan.

Susan got a promotion down at the bank; so I started taking up the slack at home. I picked up the kids at school, I washed the breakfast dishes, and most evenings I was the one who fixed dinner. I ran more errands than I used to, but that was all right because my hours were flexible.

Things are lots better, aren't they? I asked Susan one evening when we were lingering at the table after one of my better dinners. The kids were in the basement watching TV.

They're not so bad, she said, grinning off toward the dining room window in a way that I knew meant she was thinking about it. Then she got up and walked around the table, walked around behind me and ran her fingers along my shoulders. Not really so bad, she said.

I didn't mention it, but a big part of what I liked about those changes was having so many hours to myself during the day. I'd never had that experience. Hour after hour, the quiet just stretched out.

Up there in the office, I noticed how the square of sunlight from my skylight moved gradually over the floor toward me. Sometimes I just sat there, doing nothing, thinking about nothing, for I don't know how long.

Then when I did start pecking at the keyboard again, the writing went smoothly and quickly. I seemed to have composed my phrases without really having thought about them. I didn't have to force my work out the way I used to.

I began to appreciate my house. That sounds funny, I know, but you know the way you get to like a particular racquet or pair of shoes or even a court that you play well on a number of times. It was like that, except more personal. The house was like my personal friend, good company for me, helpful.

I'd stand up from the desk, walk around, come downstairs and look out this window and that, go to the refrigerator and have some juice, pick up a magazine, listen to a record.

It felt good to spend those hours home alone. It had also begun to feel safe. Until now I hadn't been able to rid myself of an old fear of being alone in the house. Of course as an adult, I'm a big enough guy, and I've kept myself in shape. But when your job has you seeing people all the time, you never really know what's going to come at you. At Sports Spot, most of the time everything had been pleasant, but there were exceptions.

Like Julie shouting at me in my office. At home, when I remembered that morning, I had to shake my head and wonder how I got through it.

I was glad to be in my own house, with the computer humming quietly and a block of sunlight just approaching my foot.

That morning, I was caught up on all my deadlines, the phone wasn't ringing, there was nothing I really had to do until three when the kids got out of school. I was getting an early jump on our Fall Membership Campaign.

I thought this must be how a Tibetan monk felt when he climbed up onto some little shelf on the side of a mountain to spend the rest of his life in the lotus position gazing down over the valley and contemplating the universe.

A noise downstairs reminded me of the one negative aspect about this working arrangement. From up on the third floor, I couldn't really hear the front or the back doorbell. If anybody came to see me on urgent business, I'd miss out on it because I wouldn't know they were down there.

But sometimes there were little noises that would catch my ear, and I'd go down to see about them. They'd be nothing but some creaking or shifting of the house. Sometimes I found that the UPS man had left a package on the back porch. But almost always it was nothing. So I tried to keep myself from being distracted and running downstairs every time I heard something.

It was like that that morning. I was in this positive state of mind and spirit. Conditions were definitely ideal. I felt that an idea was approaching, maybe a slogan for our Fall Membership Campaign, though I knew that whatever I came up with Ben would change it and then take credit for it.

But I could have sworn there was somebody else in the house. It wasn't even noise exactly but something like the floors registering weight moving across them. We've got wall-to-wall carpet in every room of the main floor and the second floor, and so you really don't hear footsteps in this house. You just sense people moving through the rooms. That sensation was making me uncomfortable since there wasn't supposed to be anybody down there.

So I went downstairs to check it out, and when I reached the second floor and turned the corner, I got a jolt of adrenaline. This figure in black was moving toward me.

Hey, Peter, it spoke, and then I knew it was Julie—her features seemed to pop into focus.

Funny, the figure had seemed huge until I recognized Julie; now she was her compact self again. She had on a black blazer, a black tank top, black tights, and black sharp-toed boots. Her hair was done up in a high pony tail, her face was pale—Julie always made a point of staying out of the sun—and her mouth was a slash of crimson lipstick.

Julie, I said, I didn't hear you come in. You scared me. I kept my voice down; I didn't want to get her started yelling at me again.

She walked right up to me, keeping her hands jammed down in the pockets of her blazer. Rang the doorbell several times, she said, staring me straight in the eye, as was her way. The door was cracked a bit. So I thought I'd better just check. Didn't want to miss you, Peter, she said, after going to all the trouble of coming over here.

What am I supposed to say to that? I said. All of a sudden it made me mad to have her walking right into my house.

Whatever, she said, smiling sort of to herself and leaning to one side to peek around behind me. Nice house you've got here, Peter. Not like I imagined it at all. You should have brought me over here. I'd have had a better opinion of you.

I kept quiet, mostly because I couldn't figure out what Julie had in mind. There's this odd thing about her, or about me and her. I'm six-two and weigh right around one-eighty; she's

understood exactly how powerful they were. To make he
op what she was doing, I would have had to steel mysel
ainst her, mentally and physically.

Raise your arms, Julie said and lightly slapped my back.
hen I did as she said, she jerked my shirt up and peeled it
er my head and arms. She let it fall.

Julie, I said.

She went on.

There was this pause. Her tank top fell to the floor beside my
o shirt.

Topless now, she walked around to face me. Julie's breasts
small and muscular. Now her nipples were sharply erect,
I I was shaken by the look of her torso. Her body was as
midating as a wrestler's.

Put your knees together, she said.

When I did, she straddled them and sat down, facing me.
continued rubbing my shoulders, except that now she also
ked on the muscles of my arms, neck, and chest. Looking
t her serious face, the hard red slash of her lips, I had the
y notion that she was extracting strength from my body.
face came nearer and nearer.

When she did kiss me, it was with a tenderness that I
ldn't have expected from Julie. For that reason I didn't
t as perhaps I might have, had she tried to force me that
too. Her thumbs brushing across my nipples, too, were
er than any touch she'd used on me so far.

ever liked you, Julie said, but in that quiet tone that was
humming. Your body was all I ever liked. Skinny, long-
led tennis player's body that isn't worth a damn for any-
 but playing tennis and sex. That's all you're good for,

hile she chanted that way to me, she pulled herself closer

five-three and doesn't weigh more than a pound or two over a
hundred. So let's say I'm almost twice as big as she is. She was
never intimidated.

I don't mean that I ever wanted her to be scared of me. But
one thing I figured out from being on the tour. Size has everything to do with the relationships. The advantage always starts
out with the bigger person, but of course that can be changed.
Little guys on the tour are always putting big guys in their
place. There weren't that many players on the tour who were
bigger than me.

I'm used to women automatically acknowledging our physical difference by how we stand next to each other or how we
look and speak, the tones of voice we use. But Julie Munroe
apparently never learned this basic principle.

At first it was annoying, the way she'd stand or sit a little
closer to me than anybody else would in a similar situation—
as if she were the larger person, and I ought to be the one to
make room. Damn nervy woman.

Then all of a sudden that way of hers got to be attractive. At
work I'd seek her out because there was this energy that came
from her, or that was generated by the two of us crowding each
other's space. The charge I got from being around her was
what started the whole thing.

But right then, in the upstairs hallway of my house, I was
back to being annoyed. Anybody else Julie's size would have
been apologizing for the intrusion. They'd be moving for the
steps to head downstairs and giving me all available slack.

Julie actually nudged me over a bit with the back of her
hand on my arm and walked past me toward the steps up to the
attic. What's up here, Peter? she asked, not turning to look
back at me.

There was that quietness in her tone that in the old days I'd learned to recognize as a signal. You want to come over to my place for lunch, Peter? she'd say in that tone.

But I could also feel how brittle her mood was. If I didn't humor her, I'd have a hundred pounds of trouble in my house.

I have a little study up there, I said. You want to see?

Without replying, she started up the narrow staircase to the third floor. Following her, I was forced to take note of her purposeful steps, her trim back, the slight swaying of her pony tail.

Around this time of day, the skylight makes my office one of the brightest rooms I've ever been in. The space is actually a small one, but when you come up into it out of that claustrophobic staircase, your immediate sensation is of having entered a large airy room.

Julie took off her blazer and casually dropped it to the floor. Maybe she thought I'd pick it up for her. I didn't.

Warm up here, she said, still keeping her back to me, walking toward the shelves as if she were taking a tour of the place. In all that light and in her black tank top and tights, her arms and shoulders looked pale as a statue's.

Have a seat, Julie, I told her. I sat down in my desk chair. Because I was so caught up with all my work, I didn't mind indulging her, but I definitely wanted to put the situation back into a proper balance.

No, I'm fine, she said, continuing slowly to pace around the periphery of the room, picking up one thing and another from the tops of my shelves. I've been thinking some about us, Peter. I thought it would be good if we talked.

Julie, I began, there's just no—

I'm not talking about starting up again! Julie spun around to face me. Rosy streaks appeared in her cheeks, on her neck,

around her collarbone. I'm talking about away then, and raised her hands as if to plu the air around her head.

I waited, but she couldn't find what she hands dropped to her sides. She turned h slightly bowed her head.

What, Julie, I said softly. Something a catching the light was about to make me fe

She spun again and stepped quickly and Turn around, she said.

What?

Just turn your chair around.

I did. I wouldn't have obeyed anybody but Julie was so obviously volatile right th to cross her unless it became absolutely n

She set her hands on my shoulders an sage that was just too familiar.

Don't do this, Julie, I said. This was h her apartment. In her quiet tone, she wo my back rubbed, and I would say yes, needed. We would walk silently toward would start. Just this way. Now her wrong, as if in busy traffic I'd suddenly driving through red lights.

Julie didn't stop. Her hands and strong, and she is a ruthless, deep-mus rubs are like no others I have ever exp yes, but almost too painful to bear. E prelude to our lovemaking.

Lean forward, Julie said. Automati we'd joked about these back-rubs bein and raised herself so that her breasts brushed my cheeks, my chin, my mouth. I confess I wanted to let my mouth respond as it ordinarily would have to Julie's doing that. I willed myself not to.

But her hand plunged down to my crotch. There wasn't anything I could do about that part of my body's response to her.

Julie, I said.

But she was smiling at me now, a clearly triumphant smile. And undoing my belt and my trousers.

Julie don't, I said, and I started to stand up.

Don't you, she said, and she actually thumped me in the ribs with the soft side of her fist. It wasn't a hard punch— maybe it surprised me more than anything else, and just slightly knocked the wind out of me. It definitely stopped me from standing up.

She went on with what she was doing. To her advantage was that she knew my body, knew what to do. I won't say that I was helpless, but I will say that Julie was in complete control of what was going on between us.

Now stand up, she said. When I didn't do it immediately, she put her hands at my neck just beneath my ears and took hold and pulled upward in such a way that I felt half afraid that she'd snap my neck if I didn't follow her wishes. I stood up enough for her to push my pants and underwear down.

Julie, I don't want this, I said, but my idiotic bobbing erection mocked my words even as I spoke them.

Stay put, she said and stood and pulled off her boots and pushed down her tights and underwear and stepped out of them. She was fast at this—there was this quick look I had of her turning in the skylight's block of light.

Then she was back at me again, straddling me, pushed up close against me and using one hand to press my head against her chest and the other to engineer what she was apparently determined to achieve.

I thought of fighting her, and I chose not to. I wish now that I had, even though I know it would have been bloody.

When she found the fit, her coming down onto me was such a shock I couldn't help calling out. I wondered if anyone would have heard my voice.

Once she had me inside her, it was as if I had become the small person and she the large. Her hands took hold of each side of my head and she pressed her breast into my face.

Your mouth, son of a bitch, she said. Use your mouth.

I wanted it over with, which was what Julie seemed to want, too, except that she was really into it. She used both me and her hand, and she came with a yelp. She pitched upward twice more before locking herself tightly against me with her body shaking. Then she pulled away and stood up, breathing hard while she stared down at me. I hated how she looked down at me, but I couldn't do anything about it.

Dumb fuck, she said.

Then she started dressing. She took her time, as if this were her place instead of mine. After a while, it was just too humiliating to sit there with my pants around my knees. I stood and pulled them up, then bent for my shirt and put it on.

I wished she had beaten me with her fists, so that I could have hated her the way I wanted to. There was nothing I could say to her, though I seemed compelled to watch her every gesture.

She used a compact and lipstick from her blazer pocket. She put them back, then used both hands to pull her pony tail tight. All the while her face and eyes ignored me. At the same time the way she moved her body told me over and over again, I had you, sucker, I had you.

Patting her pockets, looking around as if to check for any-

and raised herself so that her breasts brushed my cheeks, my chin, my mouth. I confess I wanted to let my mouth respond as it ordinarily would have to Julie's doing that. I willed myself not to.

But her hand plunged down to my crotch. There wasn't anything I could do about that part of my body's response to her. Julie, I said.

But she was smiling at me now, a clearly triumphant smile. And undoing my belt and my trousers.

Julie don't, I said, and I started to stand up.

Don't you, she said, and she actually thumped me in the ribs with the soft side of her fist. It wasn't a hard punch— maybe it surprised me more than anything else, and just slightly knocked the wind out of me. It definitely stopped me from standing up.

She went on with what she was doing. To her advantage was that she knew my body, knew what to do. I won't say that I was helpless, but I will say that Julie was in complete control of what was going on between us.

Now stand up, she said. When I didn't do it immediately, she put her hands at my neck just beneath my ears and took hold and pulled upward in such a way that I felt half afraid that she'd snap my neck if I didn't follow her wishes. I stood up enough for her to push my pants and underwear down.

Julie, I don't want this, I said, but my idiotic bobbing erection mocked my words even as I spoke them.

Stay put, she said and stood and pulled off her boots and pushed down her tights and underwear and stepped out of them. She was fast at this—there was this quick look I had of her turning in the skylight's block of light.

Then she was back at me again, straddling me, pushed up close against me and using one hand to press my head against her chest and the other to engineer what she was apparently determined to achieve.

I thought of fighting her, and I chose not to. I wish now that I had, even though I know it would have been bloody.

When she found the fit, her coming down onto me was such a shock I couldn't help calling out. I wondered if anyone would have heard my voice.

Once she had me inside her, it was as if I had become the small person and she the large. Her hands took hold of each side of my head and she pressed her breast into my face.

Your mouth, son of a bitch, she said. Use your mouth.

I wanted it over with, which was what Julie seemed to want, too, except that she was really into it. She used both me and her hand, and she came with a yelp. She pitched upward twice more before locking herself tightly against me with her body shaking. Then she pulled away and stood up, breathing hard while she stared down at me. I hated how she looked down at me, but I couldn't do anything about it.

Dumb fuck, she said.

Then she started dressing. She took her time, as if this were her place instead of mine. After a while, it was just too humiliating to sit there with my pants around my knees. I stood and pulled them up, then bent for my shirt and put it on.

I wished she had beaten me with her fists, so that I could have hated her the way I wanted to. There was nothing I could say to her, though I seemed compelled to watch her every gesture.

She used a compact and lipstick from her blazer pocket. She put them back, then used both hands to pull her pony tail tight. All the while her face and eyes ignored me. At the same time the way she moved her body told me over and over again, I had you, sucker, I had you.

Patting her pockets, looking around as if to check for any-

five-three and doesn't weigh more than a pound or two over a hundred. So let's say I'm almost twice as big as she is. She was never intimidated.

I don't mean that I ever wanted her to be scared of me. But one thing I figured out from being on the tour. Size has everything to do with the relationships. The advantage always starts out with the bigger person, but of course that can be changed. Little guys on the tour are always putting big guys in their place. There weren't that many players on the tour who were bigger than me.

I'm used to women automatically acknowledging our physical difference by how we stand next to each other or how we look and speak, the tones of voice we use. But Julie Munroe apparently never learned this basic principle.

At first it was annoying, the way she'd stand or sit a little closer to me than anybody else would in a similar situation— as if she were the larger person, and I ought to be the one to make room. Damn nervy woman.

Then all of a sudden that way of hers got to be attractive. At work I'd seek her out because there was this energy that came from her, or that was generated by the two of us crowding each other's space. The charge I got from being around her was what started the whole thing.

But right then, in the upstairs hallway of my house, I was back to being annoyed. Anybody else Julie's size would have been apologizing for the intrusion. They'd be moving for the steps to head downstairs and giving me all available slack.

Julie actually nudged me over a bit with the back of her hand on my arm and walked past me toward the steps up to the attic. What's up here, Peter? she asked, not turning to look back at me.

There was that quietness in her tone that in the old days I'd learned to recognize as a signal. You want to come over to my place for lunch, Peter? she'd say in that tone.

But I could also feel how brittle her mood was. If I didn't humor her, I'd have a hundred pounds of trouble in my house.

I have a little study up there, I said. You want to see?

Without replying, she started up the narrow staircase to the third floor. Following her, I was forced to take note of her purposeful steps, her trim back, the slight swaying of her pony tail.

Around this time of day, the skylight makes my office one of the brightest rooms I've ever been in. The space is actually a small one, but when you come up into it out of that claustrophobic staircase, your immediate sensation is of having entered a large airy room.

Julie took off her blazer and casually dropped it to the floor. Maybe she thought I'd pick it up for her. I didn't.

Warm up here, she said, still keeping her back to me, walking toward the shelves as if she were taking a tour of the place. In all that light and in her black tank top and tights, her arms and shoulders looked pale as a statue's.

Have a seat, Julie, I told her. I sat down in my desk chair. Because I was so caught up with all my work, I didn't mind indulging her, but I definitely wanted to put the situation back into a proper balance.

No, I'm fine, she said, continuing slowly to pace around the periphery of the room, picking up one thing and another from the tops of my shelves. I've been thinking some about us, Peter. I thought it would be good if we talked.

Julie, I began, there's just no—

I'm not talking about starting up again! Julie spun around to face me. Rosy streaks appeared in her cheeks, on her neck, around her collarbone. I'm talking about . . . She turned away then, and raised her hands as if to pluck the words from the air around her head.

I waited, but she couldn't find what she wanted to say. Her hands dropped to her sides. She turned her back again and slightly bowed her head.

What, Julie, I said softly. Something about her pony tail catching the light was about to make me feel sorry for her.

She spun again and stepped quickly and directly toward me. Turn around, she said.

What?

Just turn your chair around.

I did. I wouldn't have obeyed anybody else in that situation, but Julie was so obviously volatile right then that I didn't want to cross her unless it became absolutely necessary.

She set her hands on my shoulders and began a hard massage that was just too familiar.

Don't do this, Julie, I said. This was how we always began at her apartment. In her quiet tone, she would ask me if I needed my back rubbed, and I would say yes, yes, that was what I needed. We would walk silently toward her waterbed. Then it would start. Just this way. Now her touch felt profoundly wrong, as if in busy traffic I'd suddenly been instructed to start driving through red lights.

Julie didn't stop. Her hands and fingers are amazingly strong, and she is a ruthless, deep-muscle massager. Her backrubs are like no others I have ever experienced—pleasurable, yes, but almost too painful to bear. Even when they were the prelude to our lovemaking.

Lean forward, Julie said. Automatically I did so. Previously we'd joked about these back-rubs being her power move. Now

I understood exactly how powerful they were. To make her stop what she was doing, I would have had to steel myself against her, mentally and physically.

Raise your arms, Julie said and lightly slapped my back. When I did as she said, she jerked my shirt up and peeled it over my head and arms. She let it fall.

Julie, I said.

She went on.

There was this pause. Her tank top fell to the floor beside my polo shirt.

Topless now, she walked around to face me. Julie's breasts are small and muscular. Now her nipples were sharply erect, and I was shaken by the look of her torso. Her body was as intimidating as a wrestler's.

Put your knees together, she said.

When I did, she straddled them and sat down, facing me. She continued rubbing my shoulders, except that now she also worked on the muscles of my arms, neck, and chest. Looking up at her serious face, the hard red slash of her lips, I had the crazy notion that she was extracting strength from my body. Her face came nearer and nearer.

When she did kiss me, it was with a tenderness that I wouldn't have expected from Julie. For that reason I didn't resist as perhaps I might have, had she tried to force me that way, too. Her thumbs brushing across my nipples, too, were gentler than any touch she'd used on me so far.

I never liked you, Julie said, but in that quiet tone that was like humming. Your body was all I ever liked. Skinny, long-muscled tennis player's body that isn't worth a damn for anything but playing tennis and sex. That's all you're good for, Peter.

While she chanted that way to me, she pulled herself closer

thing she might be forgetting, Julie finally walked over to the staircase and gave me a final glance.

Now it's finished, Peter, she said. Her bootsteps going down the staircase were slow and loud.

In a moment I heard—or rather felt in the shaking of the attic floor—the front door slam. When I knew I was absolutely alone, I actually tried to force water to come down out of my eyes. I felt this need to let go of what I'd just been though. Crying was the only thing I could think of that might do it.

My attempts to sob sounded ridiculous. And I didn't want to do anything else I could think of. Call Susan? Call the police? Call Ben Fulton?

When I finally came down to the second floor that day, I touched the walls of the hallways and looked into my kids' bedrooms as I walked slowly past them. I ran my hand along the banister as I came down to the first floor. I was trying to think what the house must have looked like to Julie when she came into the empty foyer, figured out that I was upstairs somewhere, and decided to go up there and find me.

I set my hand on the newel post and thought hard. When I had first gone over to Julie's place, I'd followed her in, right into that immaculate living room of hers with small, framed pictures on each white wall and one bright-covered magazine in the center of a glass coffee table. I looked at all that polished wooden floor and thought to myself, so this is how she lives. She kept quiet—I did, too—while she walked me through her dining area, her kitchen, her workout space, and her bedroom. We'd said it was lunch we were there for. I stood staring down at her jungle-printed bedspread while she paced toward the window. When she turned, faced me, and asked me what I thought, I knew from her voice that the question was important, but all I could do was shrug and say, So this is where you live, Julie? While she waited for me to go on, there was a little smile on Julie's face, almost a bashful expression, but that faded. She shrugged. Yeah, this is it, she said. There had definitely been a topic there for us to discuss, but in a minute or two we'd forgotten all about it.

The Short Flight

SHE MUST HAVE NOTICED my eyes, too, because all the while we're sitting in the waiting area, we're sneaking looks at each other. Or she sees what I'm looking at—some grandly decked-out dude gliding down the corridor or a kid picking his nose and wiping it on somebody's carry-on luggage—then our eyes meet for a flurry of conversation about how I see it, too, and I know how funny it is, but you and I are the only ones who are getting this, and what does it mean?, and so on, the whole thing occurring in the catch of our eyes. She looks away, and I do, too.

Sure, everybody has this kind of thing happen to them, but what makes this communication unusual is that there's a terrific reluctance to it, as if—separately—she and I have both just renewed our wedding vows and we're doing our damnedest not to send any inviting signals to anybody, but in spite of our best intentions, here our eyes are playing that old game of peek-a-boo, I-see-you-naked, don't-you-wanta-see-me?

What else sets this experience apart from your basic airport flirtation is that in the game of age, the woman and I are advanced intermediates. Maybe we've got eighth-grade eyes, but we're both mature citizens. Neither one of us is checking into a nursing home tomorrow, but I'd guess her to be mid-forties and I know exactly how close I am to fifty.

I'm no Don Juan. Since I got married this last time I haven't gone looking to get involved with any woman. I've even taken some pains to avoid taking up with some that wanted to get involved with me. But I have this vulnerability. I don't know what else to call it. When a woman wants to be touched, I can sense it even if she and I have never met and we're in a room with fifty other people. Sometimes I can sense exactly where she'd like me to put my hand.

Call this vanity or male ego or whatever you want, the terrifying data is that there are women, attractive and unattractive, walking around everywhere who want to be touched, not necessarily by me but by some man they wish had the gumption to do it. A lot of them wouldn't admit this desire even to Satan on a dirt road late at night, and some of them would have you in a court of law early the next morning if you set that hand on them too quick or too hard or on the wrong spot. Nevertheless.

What I mean to say is that I bring a certain amount of unwilling expertise to the situation, enough so that you'd think—I'd certainly think!—that I'd be able to evade a little swirl of trouble like this. The part you can never figure, though, is old Mr. Fickle. Losing each other in the crowd, the woman and I pass through the gate and walk on board, only to find that there we are, 11A and 11B, on the two-seat side of the aisle. In the old days, if I'd been hot to start up something with her, they'd have had her in first class and me back in the tailfeather seats. But now here we are, buckling up together, the two of us fighting our natural inclinations on a sold-out commuter flight up to Albany.

How intimate you have to get on an airplane has always been a shock to me. I live in dread of some fat guy plunking his big butt down next to me, and there I'll be, snuggled up closer to him than some honeymoon couples sleep with each other. This woman isn't fat, but I get an odd notion that she has been fat—maybe until just a few months ago. She still has a few extra pounds in the middle of her body, though the cut of this very tasteful pantsuit she has on under her trenchcoat is doing all right by way of directing my attention away from her middle up toward her chest where what extra she's got looks just fine.

Something else I notice now that I'm right up beside her, there's a slight scar just along and underneath her jawbone, as if she's recently had cosmetic surgery. I'm a little clairvoyant, and I get a flash: this woman has been down; right now she's making a hell of an attempt to put herself back together.

Sometimes nowadays I surprise myself. I realize that I like her for these scars and for the weight she's lost and for the pantsuit she's picked out that makes her look good for this trip to visit her old Aunt Velveeta, or whatever. I like her for not being a suntanned blond eighteen-year-old with a smooth face, a turned-up nose, great legs and a mini-skirt that barely covers her Victoria's Secret bikini underpants. I might not want to know the details, but I like her for having lived through whatever she's lived through.

Here's what else I'm grateful for: she isn't wearing any perfume. What scent there is around her is just regular human being—clean, female, with maybe a touch of soap, deodorant, and nervous sweat. The olfactory assault of perfume always intimidates me even though I know that most women, when they're traveling, find it necessary to splash it on.

However much an expert I am on *what* women do, I'm usually as mystified as the next guy about *why* they do it. But at least in this case I know why this woman isn't wearing any perfume: she isn't looking for company. I appreciate that. I'm not either. She's window, I'm aisle, and while we're settling in, stowing our coats and her carry-on and my briefcase above and below us, we're not saying anything. We know we'll get to the conversation soon enough. Our eyes have told us we've got some things to say to each other. Whether or not we get them said is, I guess, the little buzz that has my blood pressure up about a notch and a half.

Quicker than you'd think, the plane casts away from the gate and taxis out to the runway. This, too, is unusual; I'm accustomed to sitting on airplanes waiting for take-off so long that I always start thinking of concentration camps and how all this regimented behavior and noise and machinery must be something like what kept the Jews from resisting the Nazis. You don't find any of us airline passengers unbuckling and standing up and saying, "Let me off this thing, you sons of bitches, I've had enough of this shit!" We'd probably keep sitting still, with our trays fastened and our seats in the upright position, until the flames started licking up outside the windows.

The woman and I don't say a word, though our eyes continue their subtle conversation. Even in the plane's crazy sprint down the runway and heave off the tarmac, she and I have our faces turned toward each other but our mouths shut tight. The look on her face has me wanting to put my head down in her lap.

This silence we're keeping is a cocoon we've pulled around ourselves, a private room where we're exploring each other with daring intimacy. I'll swear, it feels to me about as naughty as any act I've ever committed, and all I'm actually doing is looking at a woman who's had the good sense not to dye the gray out of her hair.

What's passing between us also has this depth to it. It's like what I imagine a lapsed Catholic must feel when he comes back to the church and confesses all his sins for the past twenty-five years. She's telling me that there was this man who brought some major-league pain down into her life, and I'm telling her that I've gone through more women than cards in a canasta deck, and until my present wife I haven't been able to find the one I've been looking for. This telling is sad as hell for both of us but all right, too, because now at least we're telling it—except that we aren't even having to say anything out loud, our stories are just flowing out of us while the aircraft rips up through the clouds toward cruising altitude.

I've lost track of time, though I guess my watch would tell me what's passed if I wanted to break the spell and look at it. But all of a sudden, there's a lurch downward of our side of the plane, we're tilted over in that direction, the plane is curving around in some spiral-like pattern, and there's a noticeable loss of power. There's also a scary quiet. The flight attendant who's coming down the aisle toward us, catches herself against a seat-back and keeps her balance, then turns and heads back to the front of the cabin, bracing herself from one seat-back to the next. I turn again to the woman beside me, her face telling me what I already know what everybody on board must be figuring out right this minute: this plane's in trouble!

What comes into me is awful, as if my vital organs are failing in unison, but there's also this curiosity about what I'm actually going to do. My third wife used to tell me she'd never run into anybody as scared of death as I am. I've never attended a funeral in my life. When my relatives and friends get sick, I don't go visit them in the hospital—I call them up and send flowers; I tell them quite frankly that just the thought of serious illness slides the backbone right out of me.

The specific occasion of my third wife's observation was this time we were on vacation, she was driving in a thunderstorm in the Poconos, and a Mayflower moving van bullied us off the shoulder and damn near over the side of the mountain. When she got the car stopped and looked over at me, I was whimpering like a four-year-old. At first she was furious—she was moody that way. "I'm scared, too," she spat out, as if I'd claimed she wasn't. Then she felt sorry for me and reached over. Her hands moving toward me released whatever inhibitions I had left: I shoved my head into her chest and before either of us quite knew what we were doing, there I was tugging at her shirt, her hand wiping the tears off the top side of my face, and her voice whispering down to me, "What has gotten into you?"

"Attendants, please carry out procedure number three. Procedure number three," comes the captain's voice over the intercom, calm enough to be informing us that we're flying over Cleveland, while beside me, the woman's face is as full of meaning as a Tolstoy novel. What she's telling me is that she sees what's in my face, which I know must be this god-awful vision of groveling cowardice.

Here's what's funny: I am aware that I ought to be strong for this woman, that she has suffered and fought despair and that she deserves someone to give her comfort in these dreadful circumstances. I lift my hands. I don't know why; it's like I want to describe the shape of something I'm about to give her, or more likely it's the gesture a frightened person makes to fend off something. Maybe you just lift your hands when you understand you're truly helpless.

Whatever my reason for doing it, it provokes the woman

beside me to act. It surprises me that I'm not surprised by what she does; her face has been telling me she's going to do exactly this. With her left hand, she catches my right hand, pulls it toward her and sets it on her breast. Doesn't do it lightly or shyly. Sets my hand right there on the front of her jacket, where anybody who wants to can see it, and keeps looking me straight in the face. The plane has been eerily quiet, but now it begins generating this low whistling noise.

My hand has had its own education. My first wife, who was only modestly endowed, used to say that if anything could have increased the size of her breasts, it would have been the palm of my right hand. She used to swear that my hands were always whispering to her chest, "Grow, grow!" So even though it seems an indecent gesture in this circumstance, my hand, of its own volition, seeks properly to grasp what it has been offered.

That movement of my fingers—and whatever else my face is telling her—provokes the woman once more. In moves that demonstrate her hands to have had some education of their own, she undoes one button of her jacket and two of her blouse, and the front clasp of her bra. She sets my hand right inside there where it wants to go. Then she rests her arm along mine, lightly pressing me against her.

There we sit, looking each other in the face and waiting. I figure we can't be that far away from what's coming to us. Up front there are a couple of women crying, and behind us there's a guy saying in this Alabama accent, "I ain't god-damn ready for this! I tell you, I just ain't god-damn ready!" The whistling noise seems to come from outside the plane and rises in volume and pitch.

Like a lock with a key turning in it, some essential part of me moves. All of a sudden—I don't know why—I'm not afraid. I feel my face relax. "What's your name?" I ask her.

"Elaine," she says. When she smiles, I know that I haven't seen her do that until this instant. "What's yours?" she asks.

First, of course, I start to tell her my name, but then something stops me, and I start to explain to her that crazy as it may sound I don't want to give her my name because this is how it has gotten started between me and a lifetime of women. I seem to be able to hear this very same exchange in all these women's voices echoing down a huge corridor, "What's yours?" and my rasping little testosterone croak, "Wayne Wilson."

I have my mouth open, and it looks like I'm going to tell her this even though I know it's going to ruin everything, but in this circumstance I'm helpless to say anything else to her.

I've gone as far as saying, "Please forgive me, but I don't want—" when the aircraft seems to catch itself and start angling upward again. It feels like when you're a kid on a swing and you've gone as far back as you can go, back to that point of weightless suspension and falling straight down, then the chains catch, you start forward and down but now you can feel the swing underneath you and you know you're going to be all right.

And it's like suddenly finding yourself frozen into a photograph of yourself doing exactly what you're doing. The plane is gaining altitude; the woman and I are sitting right there with her holding my arm close to her and my hand inside her blouse holding onto her breast like it's something precious that I'm not about to let go of. She smiles again, but I don't seem to be able to read her face the way I have been up until now. But when she makes the slightest shrug of her shoulder, I understand that well enough.

Taking my hand away, I turn in my seat and become aware of a tall blond stewardess standing in the aisle over us, trying to give us a grin. Her nametag says, "Carleen." She moves on, and my seatmate very deftly reassembles her clothing. The captain's voice comes on the intercom again, still so calm that I suspect him of being a recording; he's explaining how we've just recovered from a freak loss of power, not something that's likely to happen again in another fifty years of aviation.

With my now free hand, I touch my forehead and realize I'm sweating. As much as I don't want to, I think of my second wife, the only one of them that I never did understand why I married. Late one night while she and I were watching an American League playoff game on TV, she went completely cuckoo over the sight of Roger Clemens wiping the sweat off his brow and rubbing it into the baseball. "Why does he do that?" she asked me in a voice so shrill it was like she'd just witnessed Clemens biting a baby's wrist. I tried to explain it to her as a pitcher's ritual to bring himself good luck or something, but the truth was that even though I'd played a little baseball in high school, I didn't know why a pitcher rubbed his sweat into the ball. They just do that; I hadn't thought about it before. My explanations put her off even more. She excused herself and went to bed before the inning was over, and when I showed up a half-hour or so later, she wouldn't even turn over to give me a goodnight kiss.

So I'm sitting there looking at my sweat-slicked fingers and grinning to myself over that little harridan of a second wife I had, when Elaine's hand comes over and takes those fingers; she puts her palm right on top of the sweat. I give her a quick glance and see not a smile but something better, a look that tells me she wants me to know I'm all right with her no matter what comes next. What she does next is pretty startling: she rubs hands with me, rubbing that sweat from my brow into both our hands. When she's done with that, she gives my hand a little squeeze and lets go, gives me about five percent of a smile, then turns her face toward the window.

And that's it for Elaine and me. We don't speak, we don't touch, we don't let our eyes meet again, even after we've set down in Albany. Actually, this is Elaine's decision more than it is mine, because while we're gathering up our coats and her carry-on and my briefcase and climbing up out of our seats, my eyes are still flicking over in her direction every now and then. But now she might as well be somebody else. Just by the way she moves her body, a woman can tell you things, and Elaine's posture is definitely declaring, "I don't know you, pal."

That's OK by me, of course, because Albany is where my wife is picking me up. With a record like mine and a wife who's intensely aware of that record, I don't need even the hint of a romantic complication. I let Elaine get well ahead of me in that weird zig-zag portable corridor you have to walk through to get from the plane to the gate. From far enough back, in her trenchcoat and with her head bowed forward, she looks like Ms. Middle-aged Anybody, from Anywhere, USA, and I'm relieved about that because when I greet my wife I don't want my eyes betraying me by sneaking off to the side for one last look at Elaine.

Coming out into the public area, I don't immediately see my wife the way I'd expected to. It's a little disconcerting because there are lots of husbands and wives and sweethearts and children and parents and grandparents and friends all around waving at people coming along behind me or hugging people up ahead of me in that way people do at airports, as if they're determined to get as close as they can to somebody. I worry a second that maybe my wife has changed her hair or something and I'm just not recognizing her. I'm looking into all these women's faces, even the ones who are young enough to be my daughters, but I'm not seeing her. She'll show up, though, I'm certain of that. When I set my briefcase down in the place where I'm going to stand and wait for her, I think I hear a voice calling out my name. But then I turn and see it's just somebody else moving into the arms of his loved one.

The Reunion Joke

RANDALL IS CATCHING ME up on his views of women. Every five years he does me this favor.

Francine, he says, they know what a man's natural inclination is, they don't even argue about that.

He and I keep walking. We're back for our thirtieth, but we've snuck off from the picnic. Now we're strolling around the old high school quarter-mile track.

Randall used to run the mile.

He goes on. A man is interested in lots of women, he can't help it, that's just the way he is. But a woman persuades him that if he's really in love with her, he'll want to stay with her and only her.

He says for some reason I've never figured out, men buy into this silly do-do. It's beyond me. Randall shakes his head. He's twice-divorced. Apparently the reason he's talking to me like this is he's found a twenty-five-year-old redhead who says she'll have him.

They buy into it, he says, even though they know they're not going to love a woman but just so long. I've known one or two of those monogamous men—my Uncle William was like that, devoted as a housefly to my nasty old Aunt Gladys—but they—

Hey, Francine, he interrupts himself. He stops right there on the track.

I'm ahead of him a step or two, so I have to turn back to see him. I'm divorced, too, three years ago and I still don't like it.

Francine, he says, I want to tell you about something I did in Atlanta. I want to describe this thing to you.

Randall, I say, I've got to go back to the motel. I need my medication.

Got just the thing for you right here, he says and clasps himself. Since sophomore year this is his joke. Usually I act like I'm embarrassed, but today I'm in no mood. Let's have a look, I say.

Randall grins big as Eddie Murphy, but I can tell the idea of whipping it out in broad daylight jolts him a little. Have to wait for a more suitable time, Francine. Right now I've got to discharge some of this excess energy. It's Testosterone City around here, he says.

He takes off, just like that. A forty-eight-year-old slightly balding man running a quarter mile in his street clothes. He's just showing off, but I don't mind. Floating along on the far side of the track, he looks twenty pounds lighter than he actually is.

And I'm half-happy standing there in the cinders.

He and I have been friends since Vacation Bible School 1954—the First Presbyterian Church. Randall told me that summer was his first significant experience with erections. He claims they were my fault. They weren't. I didn't get my figure until 1956. By then I'm sure he'd had plenty of significant experience.

He just likes wild talk. I guess I must like it, too, because all these years I've been listening.

That was smart, I say when he comes up huffing and dripping. Get yourself stinked up for the cocktail hour.

Shower in your room, he says, grandly exhaling and wiping his face. While you crank up on your medication, I'll scrub down this old hard body.

Old is right, I say. And I guess it is a body. But the hard is up for discussion.

Francine, he says, throwing an arm and his manly pungence around me on the way to my car—the twenty-five-year-old redhead has his for the weekend, he claims—one thing about you is you're dependable.

He's got that right. Thirty-six years of flirtation, and I'm still putting up with him. Senior year he was always just about to give me his class ring, then changing his mind. Probably he knew that if he gave it to me, he wouldn't get it back. But I'm sick of dependable.

Randall, I say, push is just about to come to shove. Get ready.

Born ready, he says. That, too, he's been saying since sophomore year. The first look I got of my son in the delivery room, Randall's dumb words were what popped into my mind. Later on, with my daughter, the same thing, Randall not anywhere around but still yammering in my ear, saying born ready.

Francine, he says now. Can't believe that old wimp of an ex of yours supports a set of wheels like this.

I'm glad Randall has taken note of my new Celica GT, without which I wouldn't be coming back to this town.

Whether I can afford it is not the point. All my family has moved away; what dignity I'm going to have around here I have to bring with me.

I may be divorced, I tell him, but I'm not on the street yet.

Implying that I am?

Implying nothing of the kind. I'm sure none of your former classmates minds giving you rides to these reunion events. I'm sure your mom is happy to have you staying with her.

Meanness is your middle name, Francine Monahan, he says. Then he doesn't say anything else. I don't either.

In front of my door at Howard Johnson's, we still don't have anything to say, standing there in the hot sunlight trying to make the idiot key work. And I've got such a thudding in my chest.

Inside, in the cool dimness, Randall shucks his clothes like Houdini escaping handcuffs. Does it just to shock me. Won't take me but a minute, he says over his shoulder, heading for the shower. Then I'll tell you about Atlanta and we can go suck up some cocktails.

He leaves the bathroom door open, but my voice is suddenly out of order. I never saw the man naked before, and it's making me sad that I didn't when he was a boy and I was a girl. I guess it's fine enough right now to glimpse that pale back of his moving through this shadowy room, but about halfway through our junior year the sight of Randall's body was something I'd have died for. Now he's another middle-aged guy who's half kept himself in shape.

I listen to him bump around in the shower. Man takes a noisy bath. From the mess of my suitcase I dig out my medication. Now I'm wondering if maybe I took one already this morning—off my routine like this, I can't remember—but I guess two won't kill me. I go to the sink for water and plunk it down my throat.

In the mirror is a woman who doesn't look all that bad, if you understand what she's been through. Mother of two kids. Divorced wife of shithook lawyer. Radford poli sci major turned part-time bookkeeper for purposes of survival.

A guy in a Ramada Inn Lounge told me a few months ago I've got eyes that could stop a train. Doesn't take much to stop Amtrak these days I told him. I didn't sleep with him, but I did give it serious thought.

I'm trying to cost it all out, past, present, and future.

To come back here to this reunion I lost nine pounds. I look better than I have in a while and better than I'm going to. I'm standing maybe three feet away from the man I've had the hots for since the hots was something I could have. He's naked, the door to the room is locked, and if I'm not mistaken, that's a bed right over there.

I might not be as quick as Randall, but when the occasion demands it, I can step out of my clothes, too.

Shove over, big guy, you're hogging the water.

Hey, Francine, wow. I mean what's a nice girl like you—?

Don't you know how to hold somebody? Don't you know—?

I've kissed him before, lots of times, and some of it was pretty good back-seat hands-in-the-bra kind of kissing. So we're not strangers to each other's mouths. Still, with the water warming us and our skins slick and sliding against each other, this isn't something I'd trade for anything I can think of at the moment.

But you know how it is with getting what you want.

The brightest memories I have are Christmas mornings before my parents let me come downstairs and see what Santa brought. Once I had opened everything, seen it all, and compared mine to what my sisters got, the rest of Christmas was nothing but trying to pretend I was happy.

Randall asks me if I'll get pregnant.

I hope I do, I tell him, the two of us still wet, falling down onto the bed, and rolling on it. I hope to God you knock me up with twins, I say. Let's do triplets, I say. I'm pleased as a pig in mud until it occurs to me that, really, Randall is asking me if I'm going to give him AIDS or herpes.

This hurts, because I'm fool enough to be trusting him not to give me anything. I guess I could let it be my reason for saying this is a mistake, Randall. Let's just stop right here and start getting ready for the cocktail hour. But I don't say these things.

I do get pensive and have to yank on his hair a little bit and tell him no, Randall, you're not going to make me pregnant, and I'm not going to give you a disease. But let's get under these covers.

You cold?

Now who's mean? But OK, let's say yeah I'm cold. Now can we get under the covers?

You look fine, Francine. You know that? You look goddamn terrific.

This is what I want to hear, of course, but hearing it upsets me, too, because of course I know I don't even look like Terrific's second cousin. Randall is doing some sweet work with his teeth and tongue on my breasts, and here I can't forget my stretch marks.

But I'm not about to let my shame ruin these minutes.

You keep doing what you're doing, I say, and I'll just pretend I'm under the covers.

He goes on doing what he is with his mouth and making some intelligent communication with his right hand, oh some very smart messages indeed, like brushing his fingertips slowly up along the insides of my thighs. All the while, he's murmuring these things, as if he's talking to my skin, telling secrets to my body. . . . consequence of desire, he says, . . . not always known to the desiree. . . . the mind seeing paradise even when . . . animals in the forest and so on, Francine, don't you know dermatology . . . epistemology . . .

Whoo, baby, is what I'd be saying right now if I were talking at all, which I have the good sense not to be. Whoo-ooo, baby, like they sing it in rock and roll. I'm a simple person. If Randall Lewis wants to be an intellectual, that's OK by me. With my hands and my mouth and the rest of me, I'm doing what feels good. I'm alive enough for three or four people. Randall moves up over me, and I'm bringing back the dead I'm so ready for him.

Then there's a hitch in his getalong.

Francine, I'm sorry, he says.

What, I say.

I said I don't think I'm going to be able to do this.

Suddenly I see my choices laid out before me like used watches on the dusty counter of a pawn shop.

I can turn Randall over on his back and get down to work on him and try to make him a man.

I can turn myself over on my stomach and start crying into the pillow.

I can turn us both on our sides, put my arms around him and hug him and tell him it doesn't matter, I love him anyway.

Ah shit, Randall, I tell him.

Then I smack him hard right across his jaw.

I'd smack him with my backhand, too, except I know if I went that far he'd hit me back. You bastard, I yell at him. All my life you've been doing this to me.

He rolls away and holds his face. My hand stings. It occurs to me that this is what the word *aghast* means. Randall looks aghast at me. I want to hit him again, but I don't.

Francine, he says. It's not me. It's this guy. He makes a

gesture down his body, as if I want to see what's just going to hurt my feelings.

I'm getting under the covers, I tell him. And I do that. I stand up and root out the sheets, the blanket, and the bedspread. I get under there and curl up with the pillow half over my head, and I work on making my mind a blank. I can't ever remember my mind having been a blank, but that's what I want it to be right now.

Randall roots out the covers on his side, too, gets under with me, moves up beside me, and puts his arm around me, scoots up close and tries to hold me with his god-damn stupid body. It doesn't matter. I can submit to this. My mind is just about to go blank.

When you're with somebody else, you can't properly give yourself over to self-pity. After awhile I'm tired of lying in a bed with the damaged love of my youth. I haul myself up.

Come on, Randall, I tell him, let's get ready to go to this idiotic cocktail party.

I never did, he says, his face half under the bedcovers, tell you about Atlanta.

I heave a big sigh, turn on the light over the sink and the mirror, and face up to what my life has done to me. Tell me about Atlanta, I say.

Place down there called the Gold Club, he says. Spotlights and air conditioning and rock and roll so loud you have to shout over it. I'm sitting there with about two hundred other men paying eight and ten dollars a drink to see these naked women dance around on all sides of us. Wherever you're sitting, your nose is about a foot away from some woman's thigh.

I really want to hear this right now, Randall.

Francine I'm sitting there, looking right up into the bare crotch of one of the prettiest women I've ever even been in the same room with, and here is what I'm thinking. I'm thinking what kind of mind thought up this whole thing? Do they have people who actually make a living designing these places?

I turn and stare at him.

Here's what I figured out, Francine. The Gold Club might be a male creation, but there's a large portion of it—maybe as much as fifty percent—that's female. Most women don't want to be down in that audience with the men. But they want the other thing. To be up there and to be desired. To get naked and be found beautiful. And not to be touched except when they want to be.

Randall, I've got about enough of The Gold Club.

I'll admit I'm full of it, and if I'm wrong about this, then all right, I'm wrong. I can't prove it to you, Francine. But I can tell you this, I stayed there long enough to watch three different shifts of dancers. I saw a hundred women, not counting the waitresses, and I didn't see one who didn't look like she was into it.

For a certain amount of money, I say, I wouldn't mind acting like I enjoyed my work.

All right, Francine, he says, still naked and coming up beside me at the mirror, his voice half sweet and half nasty. How much money? What kind of work?

You son of a bitch, I tell him and swing at him with my hair brush. But he's too quick. I miss, and then he has me turned around holding me with my back against his naked belly and his thick arms pinning my arms.

Damn you, he whispers into my ear. You hit me again, I'm going to fuck you eighteen ways from Sunday.

Then he lets me go.

When I spin around to face him, he's grinning, and I can see why.

What does that mean, I say, Randall, stepping up to him, eighteen ways from Sunday? I give him a crisp tap on the shoulder with my hair brush.

So when we're finally through and lying there talking, Randall says you have to consummate these things.

Yeah, Randall, I say, but does it usually take thirty-six years?

Here is a conversation that does not take place. Randall, are you going to marry your baby redhead? Yes, Francine, I expect I am. I am not what you call a graceful person, but I do have the grace not to ask him that question. I expect it doesn't take much effort on his part not to volunteer the answer.

We miss the cocktail party. We discuss schemes for showing up at different times at the country club dance, but since we have only the one car, we finally decide to go together and let them say whatever they're going to.

Everybody there knows our history anyway.

I have my chin up when I walk in. I know Randall is grinning, and probably I am, too. Three or four people see us and start cheering. Pretty soon half the country club is applauding, though some of them don't know what for. I count it lucky that Billy Kincer and his video camera are elsewhere at that moment.

The dance is the most fun I've had since I was fourteen and went skinny-dipping with my cousins in North Carolina. Randall and I dance with everybody, but we keep finding each other just at the right times.

Then they stop the music and give Tim Umberger a microphone so that he can tell us stories about ourselves in the old days. Tim goes on for a good while, making us laugh the way we want to at our reunion.

Then he starts talking about Bobby Blum and Shirley Atkins, whom we had elected Cutest Couple for the yearbook. In the hallways between classes and in the Soda Shop after school and at the Friday night dances, Bobby and Shirley used to be skin-grafted onto each other. Everybody knew Bobby and Shirley parked a lot, and everybody liked to make jokes about what they might be doing.

Both Bobby and Shirley are there with us, but standing separately in the crowd with their spouses. He still lives in town, but she and her husband live in Johnson City. Like everybody else they've put on enough pounds that nobody'd call either one of them cute any more, but they look all right to me. The only kindness to aging is that what looks good to you changes, too.

Tim says he overheard Bobby and Shirley talking just a minute ago. Tim says he heard Bobby say Shirley, you look real good, how's everything going? And Shirley said, well, it's good news and bad news, Bobby. So Bobby said, all right, give me the bad news first. So Shirley said, well, Bobby, last year I had to have a hysterectomy. And Bobby said, well, that's not so bad, Shirley, you're forty-eight years old, a lot of women have to have that operation. What's the good news? And Shirley said, well, Bobby, we found your class ring.

I don't want it to, but this joke hits me hard. It's not so funny, but people are laughing like I've never heard before—I mean fall down and beat on the floor laughing. But I'm standing there feeling like somebody just opened me up and poured a bucket of scalding water down my insides.

I figure I've messed myself up by taking too much medication and then drinking on top of that. I'm ashamed of myself to be in public this way because not only can I not laugh with everybody, I'm actually starting to bawl. I'm just about to make a run for the ladies' to try to get ahold of myself, when Randall is there beside me, taking me into his arms and patting my back.

It's all right, Francine, he says, and his voice tells me what he feels. All around us, they mean to be laughing, but our fool classmates sound like the souls recently consigned to hell. Randall holds me and whispers, it's all right, Francine. I can't see his old face, but I don't have to.

DAVID HUDDLE lives in Burlington, Vermont, with his wife, Lindsey, and his daughters, Bess and Molly. He teaches at the University of Vermont and the Bread Loaf School of English.

INTIMATES

has been set in a film version of Electra by Huron Valley Graphics, Ann Arbor, Michigan. Designed by William Addison Dwiggins for the Merganthaler Linotype Company and first made available in 1935, Electra is impossible to classify as either "modern" or "old-style." Not based on any historical model or reflecting any particular period or style, it is notable for its clean and elegant lines, its lack of contrast between the thick and thin elements that characterize most modern faces, and its freedom from all idiosyncrasies that catch the eye and interfere with reading.

Printed and bound by
Haddon Craftsmen,
Scranton, Pennsylvania